DANGEROUS
PLACES
Stories

Also by Perry Glasser

Suspicious Origins
Singing on the Titanic

DANGEROUS
PLACES
Stories

Perry Glasser

winner of the G. S. Sharat Chandra Prize
for Short Fiction
selected by Gary Gildner

BkMk Press
University of Missouri-Kansas City

BkMk Press
University of Missouri-Kansas City
5101 Rockhill Road
Kansas City, Missouri 64110
(816) 235-2558 (voice)
(816) 235-2611 (fax)
www.umkc.edu/bkmk
Cover design: Vann Palmer
Interior design: Susan L. Schurman
Managing Editor: Ben Furnish
Editorial Assistant: Elizabeth Gromling
Editorial Intern: Gina Padberg
The G. S. Sharat Chandra Prize for Short Fiction wishes to thank
preliminary judges Leslie Koffler, Evan McNamara,
Linda Rodriguez, and Jane Wood.
BkMk Press also wishes to thank Alysse Hotz, Joni Lee, Shane Stricker,
and Elizabeth Uppman.

Previous winners of the G.S. Sharat Chandra Prize for Short Fiction: *A
Bed of Nails* by Ron Tanner, selected by Janet Burroway; *I'll Never Leave
You* by H. E. Francis, selected by Diane Glancy; *The Logic of a Rose* by
Billy Lombardo, selected by Gladys Swan; *Necessary Lies* by Kerry Neville
Bakken, selected by Hilary Masters; *Love Letters from a Fat Man* by
Naomi Benaron, selected by Stuart Dybek; *Tea and Other Ayama Na Tales*
by Eleanor Bluestein, selected by Marly Swick.

Library of Congress Cataloging-in-Publication Data

Glasser, Perry.
  Dangerous places / by Perry Glasser.
      p. cm.
  Summary: "Six contemporary American stories, mostly set in New York
and the Midwest, that feature characters who seek to survive as they
confront an array of dangers, from emotional fear to physical peril"—
Provided by publisher.
  ISBN 978-1-886157-69-9 (pbk. : alk. paper)
  1. Survival skills—Fiction. I. Title.
  PS3557.L348D36 2009
  813'.54—dc22
                                                        2009037713
This book is set in Miso and Adobe Caslon Pro typefaces

For the happy creatures at Moose Acres

DANGEROUS PLACES
Stories

Acknowledgements

"An Age of Marvels and Wonders" appeared in *Next Stop Hollywood*, ed. Steve Cohen (New York: St Martin's Press, 2007)

"Danger" appeared in *Phoebe*

"Fishhook" appeared in *Western Humanities Review*

"Jody's Run" contains passages from *In the Arms of Men*, which appeared in *Crescent Review* and was a winner of the PEN Syndicated Fiction Project; other passages are from "Recapitulation," which appeared in *American Fiction* Number 2, ed. M. C. White (New York: Birch Lane Press, 1991)

"Lighted Windows" appeared in the *Mississippi Review*

"The Veldt" appeared in *Passages North*

—with thanks for the generosity
    of the Virginia Center for the Creative Arts

Foreword

The novella-length first story in *Dangerous Places*—"An Age of Marvels and Wonders"—hooked me early on with a scene in a grocery store checkout aisle that is modest and almost common these days but so generous in its coloration, so present in its presentation, that I settled back in my chair for what I felt would be an engaging, rewarding read. And it was. Because the writer knew how to make the familiar behave exactly as it should in order to let his story live toward that extraordinary thing that can happen in good fiction. There is no showing off, no fancy footwork, no faking it. A voice you trust completely is completely in charge in the best possible way: "Listen," it says, "I'd like to tell you something important if you're not too busy."

And on we go, through five more stories, in the deft hands of an artist: from "The Veldt"—the collection's serious bow to the comic in our nature—to "Danger," which gathers up the book's running theme in a spectacularly fiery image of falling from the sky that nobody, looking up, truly understands at that moment except the one falling. But understanding will come. It's a perfect ending.

—Gary Gildner
Final Judge
G. S. Chandra Prize for Short Fiction

An Age of Marvels and Wonders

The man pinned between my car and my neighbor's house screamed at first, shouted, threatened, cursed, bargained, pleaded, then finally wept, but now that he is quiet, I risk a close look. My car door strikes the gray stucco wall. The space in which I can maneuver is only a few inches because the driveway is so narrow. Taking my time, I emerge by first extending my neck and head. After I push my left arm and left leg out, I raise my arm to the sky, twist, turn, and my right arm and leg follow. The driveway is that tight.

In the dark, cold rain, it's difficult to see much of anything. Twenty-five yards up the street, just beyond the oak that dominates the block, a streetlight sputters, but we are in dark shadow. Wind rustles the wet leaves; shadows shift. This neighborhood is known for its tree-lined streets, shallow lawns, driveways, and pitched roofs with old-fashioned vinyl and cedar shingles. Close to campus on this side of the river, housing is modestly dense. Despite the rain, the air carries the sweet smell of fireplace smoke. People like living here.

The man is bent forward at the waist, sprawling across my car's trunk, his arms wide, his right cheek flat on the black metal, his mouth open. He mumbles, but I'm damned if I can make out what. The fussy wind disturbs the trees. Leaves sigh and shake. Thunder grumbles far off, but I see no lightning. By morning, horizontal rain and wind will strip the last leaves off the trees. But not yet. A heavy whirling mist makes nothing distinct. My driveway is suddenly a dangerous place.

The young man is tall and thin, near haggard, but that's a fashion statement, not the sign of hardship. We've met. We're old friends, he and I. Men of the world, he thinks, the kind that share understandings of work and women. I have a well-honed imagination, but I can't explain how the short woman ever became involved with this man. Just a guy with a baseball cap and a mullet. What could that mean? His cap brim is tight and low over his eyes. He tries to push himself erect, but his hands slide feebly on the wet metal. The crimson satin baseball jacket might be new. He's an Expos fan. Red, white and blue, but Canadian, a team that no longer exists, for God's sake. There's devotion, for you. The sleeve is ragged and torn where it snagged on the wall. I draw close enough to see from across the car that he is breathing, so I gingerly slide back into the driver's seat, race the engine, and put the car into reverse.

That causes me to back into him, another mistake. It's not panic; I am just a confused old man. I go forward a bit and straighten my wheels, but as I back out the length of the driveway, I oversteer and my car's front left fender crumples sickeningly when it scrapes the wall. My headlight shatters.

The amber turn lamp falls intact out of its socket, dangling from black-taped snakelike electrical cords.

All told, I've run the young man down three times. How can the short woman forgive me?

I manage to back out as far as the street, but as my rear wheels find the road an SUV coming much too fast from my right brakes and then skids past my driveway, barely missing my car. Kids. Who else is that fearless on wet macadam? The insistent bass of their radio fades as they fishtail dangerously before straightening out and running the corner stop sign. They should be more careful. On a night like this, accidents happen in a heartbeat.

The young man collapses to the ground in the oblong spot cast by my remaining headlight. My windshield wipers work fine, so I can see him plainly. For a crazy moment, I think diamonds and rubies and gold surround him, but the gems are only shards of glass and plastic that sparkle with reflected light. His cap falls. Saturated by rain, it becomes shapeless and limp.

My Ford straddles the sidewalk, rear wheels in the street, front end in the driveway. I must have run over him if he was behind the car and now is in front, right? I suppose I could have steered forward to where the driveway aprons at my garage, but I am confused. At least he is no longer pinned against the wall. From within the car, I can't see well enough to know if he bleeds. The crimson jacket is blotted with dark spots, sure enough, but that could be from rain, not blood. Just as likely, the dark spot is yet another betrayal by my weak eyes. Then again, he could be bleeding internally. If an artery is severed, he'll bleed out pretty quickly. This is an urgent situation.

He moves and groans. One of his legs is bent under and away from him in a way no leg should bend. I shut the engine and extinguish my remaining headlight. It's easy to open the door now. I walk toward him, but then change my mind. Instead, I go directly into the house. I tap in 911.

Once I give the dispatcher all she needs to know, I sit on a stool at the table in my dark kitchen's breakfast nook. I dry my hair and neck with a dishcloth until the pulse of a red and blue strobe douches the night. As I open my front door, I lift my old woolen jacket from a wooden peg, shrug into it, step onto my enclosed porch, and push my screen door out as far as the spring will allow it to go. Wet wool. That's an aroma all about manly action. I should have a Labrador retriever. Duck lures. Things like that. I lean into the night and welcome the cool rain to my flushed face. Two policemen in rubber storm gear holding long flashlights hurry up my walk.

Almost a year earlier, two days before she follows me home, the short woman stands ahead of me in the checkout aisle. She is short like you could put her in your pocket, but she is hardly a dwarf. Just short. She glares at me. She says, "No," biting off the word, bitter on her tongue.

The cashier is none too happy with me, either.

I offer the short woman money because I'm hoping that for five or ten dollars I can save myself thirty minutes and score points with God. I am not looking for some medieval indulgence here, no Get Out of Purgatory Free card, but just maybe if the Good Lord wills it, a small miracle, say some July day my sandals might be guided past the bubblegum. All I want is to pay for my Muenster cheese, the soft kind. It will go with the unpretentious Riesling chilling in my refrigerator at home. I like the tapered neck of the brown bottle. The label with the milkmaid and the cat and the woodcutter pleases my eye. On impulse, I've picked up some Rye Crisps, something to vary from my usual Ritz. Rye Crisps: my low-threshold adventure of the week.

My entire purchase is my entire dinner: cheese, crackers and a glass of sweet yellow, German wine. Maybe two glasses. My doctor would kill me about the cheese. She'd give me a long, scary lecture. Then I'd go home and regret I had not bought a creamier Camembert.

The short woman is not slow. She pushed a full cart to the register, and she took only a minute or two to empty it, her hands darting swift as nesting birds. She's entitled to the time; I am not impatient; I have no place to go and no one waits for me. The only problem is she doesn't have enough money.

The cart also contains her kids. They ride with the groceries. That's not unusual. Lots of people do that. It's a long sight better than the ones who lash the kids to their wrists with clothesline. These two might be a boy and a girl; it's hard to be certain. One wears a pink nylon jacket and the other wears a blue nylon jacket. You don't need to be Charlie Chan to figure this family out. The boy is four, tops, closer to three. The girl, maybe six. The frayed stitching on the jackets' quilting is unraveling, and on the girl's chest a dirty tuft of the fill leaks. The kid picks at it like it was a polyp. Beneath their unzipped jackets they wear candy-colored striped T-shirts and generic jeans with lots of room to grow, the cuffs rolled up. They are roiling around on each other, squirming, needy, whiny, and loud. Their identical black knit hats stretch almost over their eyes, and they both have thick-knit maroon mittens clipped to the sleeve ends. Outside in early March, it is still cold enough to mist breath, but inside? There's no need for woolen hats, so both kids are pink with heat and shine with sweat.

They have crusty, chapped running noses and what might be the glistening remains of a couple of purloined lime lollipops rimming their lips. They strain to touch their mother. The boy says, "Uppie uppie uppie uppie," a shrill mantra that in the past must have gotten him lifted into his mother's arms. It doesn't work right now. On and on he goes, like a dentist's drill through Novocain. The girl's sticky hands pull at her mother's breast, yielding beneath a stained yellow sweatshirt. The neckline stretches; we all see the pink strap of Mom's ratty bra and the delicate line of her clavicle under translucent skin.

Beth Anne, our cashier, has efficiently pushed the little mother's groceries over the register scanner. Beth Anne languidly chews gum, her mouth slightly open, and though her hand has twice drifted to the post to switch on the Problem Light to bring Frank the Manager, she has not flipped it yet. She touches her nameplate and rolls her eyes, at sixteen having seen from the vantage point that is Register 4 all life has to offer.

Jaded Beth Anne is destined for better things. Beth Anne's chronic impatience for her real life to start has already chiseled frown lines in her young face. Despite all she has discovered about herself since she was eleven, the details of her bright, glowing future remain indistinct. All she knows is that as long as her skin stays clear and she keeps away from the Debi Cakes and Ding-Dongs, she'll be fine. Perfect, in fact.

I don't try to be judgmental, but ever since Dr. Feldman told me that macular degeneration would sooner or later leave me blind, I see more. It is one thing to be in the world; it is another to see it. What I do not see, I fill in. It amuses me.

The blank spots in my eyesight may spread, but the mind supplies superior vision.

Look at Beth Anne, for example. The knowledge of her Special Destiny is why trailer-trash loser-mothers plunge her into despair; they are irritating reminders of the capriciousness of Fate. She is not going to think about that. No sir. Customers are spittle afloat in the clear pool of her existence.

Look at the short mother, for another. Payment is due. $177.58 worth of groceries. She is down to searching for coins. Most of us want to avert our eyes at such a time; we read checkout aisle literature—pondering the aliens that, despite monitoring TV and radio broadcasts for generations, choose not to appear to world leaders in the company of diplomatic envoys, but instead taunt us by causing cellulite, arthritis and the rare form of leukemia that puts boys in bubbles; we read about the talking dog in Guatemala that in perfect English has predicted the end of the world for Tuesday next; we're enchanted by winners of the genetic lottery for whom fame and fortune do nothing but plunge them into heartbreak and life-dramas filled with pathos so much more acute than our own, suffering the curse of being gorgeous, talented, or God-forbid rich. We wonder what the fifteen secret new ways to have sex that are guaranteed to keep a man faithful could be. Where is this research conducted? How long has it been going on? Can they use a near-blind sixty-two-year-old subject? Are we certain the camp followers of Caesar's legions were ignorant of these techniques? How about the courtesans who flourished in the Kremlin at the time of Catherine the Great? Fourteenth-century geishas? Have they checked the carvings on Hindu temples in Burma? Fifteen new sex techniques. Think of it.

Oh, we are lucky to live in an Age of Marvels and Wonders, an age of daily miracles that inexplicably cannot ascertain why fatty deposits swell behind the retina. Maybe the aliens know, but choose not to tell us. Perhaps they are the cause. Perhaps we should journey to Guatemala to ask the dog.

The little mother dumps her purse onto the checkout counter. An errant nickel rolls free like an illegal immigrant sprinting across the Rio Grande, but the little mother slaps it flat. She pushes a single finger through the pile of crumpled pink tissues, a rainbow-colored kerchief, one of those clever, clear-plastic rain bonnets that once unfolded never seem to be able to be put right again, four postage stamps, an open roll of butterscotch Lifesavers, a knobby hairbrush, two lip-sticks, what might be a tampon holder, maybe a dozen keys on a single key ring, two pointless pencils, one of those fat pens with four different color points, Sunday giveaway food coupons that are irrelevant to today's purchases, a bus sched-ule, one half of a crumbling Lorna Doone cookie, and three packets of McDonald's ketchup.

I do like to account for details.

The little boy has already torn open his box of Animal Crackers.

Mom's fingers tear at her sky blue nylon wallet. She probes compartments. She separates Velcro. The thing is jammed with crumpled slips of paper and folded photos, but none of that crap is money. Money is what she needs. Money is what I offer.

"Let me buy the little boy the cookies. It will be my plea-sure. A gift." I ask Beth Anne, "How much more does she need?" and the cashier's eyes cloud. Why is this old fool ask-ing her to perform subtraction? Beth Anne's inchoate glow-ing future does not include higher math. Eyeliner, yes. Body piercing and tattoos, of course. She already gives head better than Paris Hilton, not much of an achievement, but Beth Anne's only evidence are the swiftly achieved moans of Frank the Manager. But subtraction?

"You saying you don't want nothing?" the little mother says to me.

I say, "It's a loan. Or pass it forward. Whatever works for you." I withdraw a ten from my wallet. It has several older and younger brothers snug and warm beside it. I live alone, my needs are simple, and the pension is adequate. I am not flying to Australia any time soon, but I can open and enjoy a bottle of Riesling. She can see the bills. The ten I offer her is crisp.

"A loan," she repeats, and snatches the money from my fingers without touching my hand. "A loan."

Beth Anne taps a few buttons. The register bursts open. Beth Anne hands me $5.42. I gesture it goes to the little mother, but Beth Anne hands it to me, anyway. This means the little mother won't have two spare cents on her as she makes her way home, but by the time I drop my Muenster onto the rubber belt that feeds everything across Beth Anne's magical laser scanner, the young mother is gone. If she suffers a flat tire, she will have to barter Doritos for assistance. Beyond Register 4 and the magisterial Beth Anne, I figure I am done with miracles for this day.

But outside, I see the little mother beside a red pickup truck just two spaces away from my black Ford Taurus. This is how strange life can be; despite several acres of parking spaces, Chance makes us neighbors.

The kids are strapped into their car seats. The truck motor runs and the groceries are secure beneath a restraining elastic net in the pickup's bay, but when she sees me open my car's door, she comes over. With her fists on her hips, she says, "You don't buy me so cheap."

She should have gloves, I think. "I'm not trying to buy you."

She snorts.

"Not that cheap," she repeats and returns to the truck. She struggles to haul herself up behind the wheel. It's an extended cab, just large enough to have a back seat where the kids are strapped in. The engine roars as she drives up the rpms, so when she jerks it into reverse, she pops the clutch and the tires grab the macadam. They spin and smoke before she steers to the parking lot exit. By then, despite the cold, the truck exhaust is colorless.

Buy her?

The Riesling turns out to be more challenging to the palate than I'd expected; it's respectable, though a long way from distinguished. As I slice the cheese to precise proportions of a Rye Crisp, I reread *The Magic Mountain*, Thomas Mann's doorstop of a novel. I am at the wonderful passage about Old Castorp's silver baptismal bowl, that symbol of propriety, the family's station in life, and the continuity that is about to be disrupted by History. The irony is exquisite; we know how events will engulf the family, while the family, of course, does not. The print is small, but if I hold the book close to my face, I have no trouble. I read while the university's classical music station plays the usual pleasant, undemanding material. Tchaikovsky. Berlioz. Mozart's shorter pieces.

I used to teach a night class at our fine second-tier state institution. We are proud of our basketball and football teams, manic about wrestling, and the trustees and senior administrators point proudly to the university's mission of serving the citizens of the state. True, the students are not always of the most astonishing quality, though they are willing enough.

The chair of the Business Department is new. Young, hired away from a school back east, he was no doubt lured by our superior public schools and inexpensive housing. I suppose he has children or is planning to. I hardly know him, but he called a few months ago to ask if I could once again offer my winter session night class. The department secretary supplied him with my name. She keeps the Rolodex.

"Do you have any available day sections?" I asked.

Well, no, he did not. Only regular faculty teach day classes. I had to turn him down. He thanked me, did not ask me why I was uninterested, and told me he'd call if the situation changed.

I miss teaching. My class in Finance for Non-Finance Majors began on the very first night with my writing on the chalkboard in letters a foot high,

ASSETS = LIABILITIES + EQUITY.

We then spent fifteen weeks exploring what that means. It's as practical as swine science and has many more applications.

Last year, the last time I taught, I had a nice group. At 9:30 at night, after class, one or two earnest students in their twenties often walked beside me to the parking lot over the winding footpaths that lace the campus like fine wrinkles above an old woman's smile.

They'd ask the most extraordinary questions, seeking advice on credit card debt, mortgages, equity loans, life insurance, bankruptcy, and even sometimes retirement planning. Inevitably, their questions about personal finance led to my questions about their lives, and that's when I'd learn about sickly parents, untrustworthy spouses, too many children, rotten bosses, bad spending habits, thwarted ambitions, sudden medical bills, and unobtainable dreams. I'd hear of husbands with all the financial restraint of teenagers; young wives who read magazines that told them they should want to "do it all" and felt guilt that they could not, and did not even want to.

My counsel mattered. I'd say, "Why not stay home with the kids for five years?" and you'd think they'd been granted a license to follow their heart's desire. As if they needed one. But here was hard evidence. The professor told them only what they already knew: they were wearing themselves out and doing their kids no favor.

I'd hear it all in that quarter-mile walk. At 10:00 P.M., when the bell tower clock chimed, those leaden notes rolled over us, a signal to stop chatting and head home. But we'd always linger to prolong our sense of embracing peace, cupped in the silence beneath the splendor of winter's starry sky and the globe of the final bell tone expanding outward over the entire prairie. Our footsteps broke the frozen crust on the snow. When we glanced back, we saw where we had passed.

Last year on just such a night, I said to a twenty-seven-year-old woman, "Be more aggressive with your savings and don't let the money your mother left you stand idle." She was terrified of an inheritance. Too many zeroes. "You've paid off your credit cards?" I asked, and when she said that she had, I suggested she undertake risk via the stock market. "Youth is a great advantage," I said. "Time will heal any bad luck. Look, you owe it to your mother that her future grandchildren will afford college and grow up in a nice house. Isn't that what she wanted?" She nodded. These were the things she needed to hear.

She walked with me all the way to my car and helped me brush an inch of powdery snow from the windshield and rear window. As I climbed into the driver's seat, she said good-night, and that's when I nearly killed her.

I'd turned around in the driver's seat. I'd checked my mirrors. I backed out very slowly. I backed out of my parking space and when she cried out stopped just six inches shy of running her down. Never saw a thing.

My night vision, I learned, was deteriorating faster than day. Macular degeneration is a funny thing. No one understands it. I've got idiopathic spontaneous drusen, which means that for no known reason in no predictable pattern and at no predictable rate, crap accumulates in tiny spots beneath my retina.

Try planning your life around "idiopathic" and "spontaneous."

I finished the semester, but I could no longer kid myself. I'd become a hazard. In daylight, I compensated by moving my head as I drove. Constantly changing perspectives helped. I suppose I could simply have hired a car service—teaching hours are regular enough—but the idea is humiliating. My doctor said I was still OK to drive, but not to kid myself, either. Bright sunshine, only.

Besides, I do not need to teach. At least, not for the money.

For twenty-four years I worked for Great Plains Doll & Figurine. I still have my office door plaque: Mr. Robert Evans, CFO. Every woman under fifty owned a Birthday Betty. But when Mr. Feinstein died, his sons, those blockheads, exported core processes to Brazil and south Asia. When the word spread that Birthday Betty had her hair curled and lipstick painted by nine-year-old Malaysian orphan girls who worked fourteen-hour days, the company tanked. My pension...forget it. Not too bad because I took an early cash buyout, but it's not what it should have been, either. As I said, adequate until I go blind. Then I can implement my exit strategy.

Jeanne, my wife, was the real teacher in our family: an anthropologist. Summers she would travel to the most obscure places on the planet while I balanced books and tended to payrolls. Ovarian cancer burned through her like prairie fire in drought. Once Jeanne was gone, I could think of several reasons to leave, but where would I go?

So I will die here. Nowhere else.

Midwestern college towns have their charms. True, snow is not one of them, but the movie theater is first rate and I never stand in line to obtain a ticket. Live theater at the university means a new production nearly every week except for summer; *King Lear* last year was first rate. Our bookstore serves coffee with cinnamon or nutmeg, and they load the fireplace with hardwoods. Cybele, the older woman who owns the place, calls me "Professor." I hold her magazines closer and closer to my face, and she never makes me buy them. The letters appear to shimmy and dance. When the dark spots grow too large, I will say farewell to books. If I have the courage, I will say farewell to everything else, as well.

I rinse my glass and replace the remainder of my cheese into my refrigerator. I own a set of plastic containers in all shapes and sizes for such leftovers.

I think: Buy her? Buy her? What could she mean, buy her?

Tuesday, after a chicken sandwich at lunch, I head for the market, but I don't see the little mother. I like fresh produce, and I am out of lettuce. But on Wednesday the little mother sees me in the parking lot before I see her. I really wasn't looking for her. Not really. I often go to market.

She comes right up to me and says, "I don't have your money."

"That's all right," I say. She really is short. Her head comes to my chest.

Her hands are deep into her back pockets and she stares at the ground near my feet. It makes her seem earnest. She wears the same mustard-yellow sweatshirt, faded jeans, and brown boots as when I first saw her. Her chin is a hard line, her jaw set, and when she turns her head, I see her fine profile. Without children pulling at her, she is pretty. Translucent white skin, pink and radiant with inner light generated by the cold and her inner heat. I recall the glimpse I had of those bird-thin bones of her chest when her daughter grabbed at her breast.

"I might have it in a week. I have a thing happening, and if it works out I will have your money." We walk beside each other toward the market's entrance. "It was kind, what you did. It was kind. Are you a kind man? I need to know if you are a kind man."

"I'm fifty-seven," I lie.

She nods. Her hair is tied back. I don't know how women do that. Oh, I realize it is all rubber bands or elastic, but the knack of it is something more. Jeanne never did it. Her hair was full and loose and brown, and she gave it one hundred brush strokes every night before she went to bed, but that did not stop it from falling out from the chemo. The little mother's hair is red; not bright red, but red like burnished copper. Her eyes are sea green.

"My kids are with my sister," she says. The electric-eye door of the Stop 'n' Go swings inward for us, but we stand in the cold. It shuts and opens, shuts and opens, because we are right in the sweet spot that makes the electric eye crazy. "That's me over there," she says and points to the bulletin board in the Stop 'n' Go's entranceway. "That's what I have going on."

We walk closer. She shows me a sheet of paper that reads, *Housekeeping. Reasonnable Rates.* Along the sheet's bottom she has neatly penned her phone number on a dozen or so small slips scalloped from the main sheet so they may be torn off one at a time. The little mother has done her work with a computer that, she tells me, is at the library. They charged her a quarter for the green card stock. The page is headed by a graphic of a mop and pail. I don't tell her she has misspelled a word, and I solemnly tear her phone number from the sheet and place it in my shirt pocket. "There," I say. "I am first. I hope it brings you luck."

"You are a kind man," she says. Some people smile with just their lips; some with their lips and maybe their eyes, but the little mother smiles with her whole face. It is something to see. Her teeth are crooked but otherwise fine. She tells me I am kind as if she were a prospector who discovered gold. She says, "I have to leave now. Lynette is not really my sister, just a good friend. I miss my blood, but they are far off and gone, so I make my own family."

"What's your name?" I ask.

Her lower lip curls inward and she chews it, as if she is thinking. "Call me Raylene," she says. "The name on my license is Raylene Goodheart." She looks at me as if expecting a challenge.

Her red truck is parked far off. It's huge, the Dodge diesel, she tells me. Raylene walks quickly away, nearly running. Her copper-red hair flounces as she runs. Her hair is why her skin seems so pale. I can still see her distinctly when she pauses, turns, and pulls her hands from her rear pockets to wave to me. She probably had freckles when she was a kid.

Goodheart, I think. I almost believe it.

I buy a tin of cashews, a new hairbrush, a small bottle of Old Spice Aftershave, and after thinking about it, I buy Grecian Formula, the blue goo in a tube for graying hair. It's not a dye or anything, but it enhances a man's mature look. The aroma is lavender. It's masculine. What can it hurt?

I am most of the way home when I see the red truck in my rearview. I pull into my narrow driveway, and as I walk from my car across the untidy front lawn to the front door I pretend I do not see Raylene has followed me home and sits in her idling pickup.

Two days later, twelve of the fifteen slips with Raylene's phone number have been torn from the forest-green sheet at the Stop 'n' Go. I stand close to count them. The day after that, Raylene's announcement is hidden beneath a yellow-poster about the formation of a soccer league for girls ages eight to twelve. I have never thought how this bulletin board speaks the life of this community. I stand close enough to read. A used snowplow is for sale. Someone collects money for African orphans. These lives are real, not my fabrications to fill in blanks. I've never looked. A new church is form-ing. There are announcements: childcare, résumé preparation, support groups for abused women, for alcoholics, for children of alcoholics, offers of jobs and free kittens, tutors for the SATs, people who want to stay still selling cars and trailers to people who want to travel. There is no support for anyone going blind.

I rearrange some thumbtacks to give Raylene more vis-ibility, but just a few days later, her ad is gone.

One morning before I have my oatmeal and toast, Raylene appears at my front door. I have not yet shaved. I'm wearing a T-shirt and tan slacks. She stands wordlessly on the three cement steps, looks up at me, then walks past as though she has been invited and there is just no question of what must happen next. As she passes the doorframe, she sidles to make room between us for her plastic carryall filled to overflowing with cleansers, rags, paper towels, glass cleaner, Endust, and lemon-scented furniture oil. She has pulled her hair back with the scrunchy thing again, and in her dirty flat-soled canvas sneakers, she is even shorter than I thought before. Even tied back, her hair hangs lower than her collar.

She makes a second trip to the red truck, and as she passes me again she says, "Nice place. Coffee would be good." She is halfway up the stairs when she calls over her shoulder, "I hope you own a vacuum."

She starts in the upstairs bathroom. Her pants are scarlet. They call them capri pants today, but I called them pedal pushers, once. Jeanne owned a pair, thin sky-blue cotton. She wore them when she was a girl. I may go blind, but I will always be able to see that.

The summer we met, Jeanne was on a red and white three-speed girl's Schwinn with a big brown leather seat, fenders on the wheels, and pink and white streamers that fluttered from the handlebars. We were kids. She buckled a white wicker basket over the front wheel, and she loaded it with food and a gunmetal gray steel thermos so we could ride together to Harris's field where we picnicked beneath a willow, the only tree in that field. Toward evening, the mosquitoes came up awful, but that afternoon was the first time we kissed. Jeanne's lips were salty. Neither of us closed our eyes, we were so damned eager to see.

"My neighbor has the kids," Raylene calls down to me, shouting over the roar of water in the bathtub. She is filling a zinc pail. "I only have two hours," she shouts. "The thing I said. It's happening, but not fast enough. I cannot pay you money. Do you mind ammonia?"

"You don't have to do this," I shout up to her as I measure out the coffee and try to remember if the bathroom soap has my pubic hair on it.

The water stops running. Her head appears over the balustrade. Just her head. "Yes, I do," she says, "I do have to do this." When she steps back her head vanishes, but then reappears. "I should know your name," she says. "You should tell me your name."

"Bob."

"Bob," she says. "Bob is good."

Later, after she asks if it is all right if she stands on one of my wooden chairs, I watch as she wipes grime from the refrigerator's top. Her shirt rides up, and I see that across her back she has that tattoo, a curlicue of some kind from kidney to kidney. It looks Gaelic.

I notice this tattoo on many young women. It is not as though I am inspecting. It is the fashion. They wear short shirts to bare their midriffs, and they wear low-rise jeans, so when they turn or move I can't help but notice the tattoo. They are none too careful about appearances in front of an invisible man, though I am beginning to allow myself to believe that for Raylene, I may no longer be invisible. The tattoo is ubiquitous. For all I know, my daughter in Australia has such a tattoo.

Two hours later, Raylene sits at my kitchen table. She drinks a second cup of coffee. "This is what I do," she says. "but I am sorry I did not get to finish. I can vacuum another time."

"I must pay you." When she does not argue, I find a twenty. "Is that enough?" I ask, and Raylene says that this time it is, but if I want her to come back, she will need to charge me regular rates. That seems fine to me, and we shake hands. Her tiny hand is rough from housework.

As she stands, she touches my bookstand on the kitchen table. Some people who are alone have a TV. I have my bookstand. It is a chrome tubular thing designed to hold a book open and erect, allowing me to keep my hands free while I read. I want to read as much as I can before I cannot read anymore.

"That's a big book," Raylene says. "Are you going to read all of that?"

"I've already read it. I am reading it again."

She stares at me as if to see if I am making a joke at her expense, but then she says, "Like Scripture?" and I say, "Yes. But it is not a holy book. Some books are worth a second and third look."

Her finger touches the page, drawing back her hand as though she has touched something sacred. She lifts the heavy book from the stand, and her lips move when she reads the title, *The Magic Mountain*, but then she sits again and, aloud, she flawlessly reads:

"Then, seventy-five years ago, I was the youngster whose head was held over this selfsame basin; that was in the dining-room too, and the minister spoke the very words that were spoken when you and your father were baptized, and the clear water flowed over my head precisely the same way—there wasn't much more hair than there is now—and fell into this golden bowl just as it did over yours." Her eyes shut; she seems to be considering something far away and long ago. "I cannot abide Baptists," she says. "Were you baptized?"

I nod. I add, "When I was a baby. My children were not. It did not seem important."

"I did not see any photographs of children," she says, and though she does not ask, I tell her about Geoffrey in Manhattan and Irene in Sydney. I don't like to visit Geoffrey; I tried it once. There is nothing to do in New York City except hurry to the next overpriced restaurant. If Irene could have settled on the moon, I think that's where that girl would have gone. She could never travel far enough away. "Irene and her mother...something was wrong there," I say, and Raylene nods as if she recognizes an old story. I do not mention the seven-year-old grandson I have never seen.

Jeanne flew eighteen hours to Sydney to stay three months when the baby was born, but I stayed here. From Chicago to San Francisco to Hong Kong to Sydney. Think of it. The world in a day.

"The photo on the bedroom bureau. That's your wife?"

"Was," I say. "Jeanne."

"Pretty woman. They used nice wedding dresses in those times. They call that kind of brown finish *sepia*, right?"

"Yes."

"Like henna rinse, but on a photograph. The veil she wore; it's pretty. That's called a mantilla, isn't it?" I say that it is. Raylene purses her lips. "I thought I was born again when I was fifteen. I gave my life over to Jesus Christ Almighty. Everybody was doing it. I will not argue that good can come of it, but I was knocked up six weeks later." She laughs as she washes our coffee cups and places them in the proper cabinet. "So much for the power of prayer. I have made a deal with the Lord that if He stays out of my life, I will stay out of His, provided He watches over my children. I hope that does not shock you."

I tell her it does not.

"It would, some." Her green eyes flash to my bookstand and she says, "I read a lot to my kids. It's important."

I tell her I agree. "Tell me about the tattoo on your back," I say.

"It's my tattoo," she says after hesitating. Have I been too personal? "I don't know about other people. Mostly I see girls with Celtic knots. They'd be Irish, I guess. But mine is the symbol of Albania. I found it in the encyclopedia. It's a two-headed falcon with a crown. My grandma was from Albania." She stands up and turns her back to me, lifting her shirt just enough. "I just love it."

And then she quickly gathers up her carryall tray of cleaning stuff. Since I live alone, she thinks she should only have to be at the house twice each month, a fact that will make her schedule difficult, though she is willing. I ask her to come once each week, anyway. She shrugs. "There's always work to be done," she admits. "I don't do laundry, though," and I agree to her terms. No laundry. She will do windows every other month or so, "But not in winter." Fifty dollars, cash, each week.

She asks me to put in some supplies—more paper towels, rags, Murphy's Soap—and she will leave everything in a plastic bucket in my garage.

I buy a better vacuum for the upstairs carpets. An upright would be awkward for the short woman, so I buy one on casters. It's a tradeoff between power and weight with these things. The vacuum is made of an alloy created by NASA. Is that a miracle, or what? It costs nearly $400, but who cares?

Each week, Raylene cleans my kitchen and both bathrooms, and every other week she vacuums. The little unit follows the little woman like a greedy puppy. She is careful not to let it collide with the furniture. The first time she vacuums under my bed, as we sit over our coffee she asks, "Why do you have a baseball bat under your bed?"

"I forgot it was there. Is it still there?"

"I moved it to your closet. It was in my way. Do you need it under the bed?"

"The closet is fine." Houses breathe at night, but Jeanne was sure every creak and sigh was a burglar. She would not abide a firearm, but she insisted I keep the baseball bat. It is a genuine, wood, Louisville Slugger. Pondering blindness, I wish I'd insisted on a gun.

From time to time, Raylene takes care of other things. She wipes mirrors. She dusts. She washes crystal. She kneels to wipe dust from the decorative carvings on the bedroom furniture. She oils the mahogany pieces in the bedroom, and the oak pieces in the living room. Raylene informs me that once it gets warmer she will have to spend a day doing nothing but my upstairs windows, but on another day she will do downstairs. "It's amazing you can see anything at all outside," she says with feigned pity. "They are awful dirty and awful dim. Don't you ever want to look outside?" With my permission, one day she climbs a chair and disassembles the glass prisms of the fixture over the dining room table. She washes each piece in a bucket of soapy water. When she is finished, she flips the light switch. "Isn't that fine?" she asks with satisfaction, and I agree the room is brighter, though I cannot tell with any certainty.

Raylene is grateful when I buy her a white enamel folding stepstool. It's lightweight, and when she stands on it, she can near touch the ceiling. When she admires what a good idea the stepstool is, I tell her she can have it. I have to persuade her to take it, but she agrees when I point out her other customers will be happy if she does not stand on their furniture.

She works three hours each Tuesday, and she always takes the time to share coffee and talk when she is through. She usually stays an hour more. "Do you chat with all your customers?" I ask.

"Do I look crazy to you, Bob?" she says and helps herself to milk. She finds sugar, as well.

Her business grows. First, they stop watching her every move; then they trust her with a house key. She is able to clean more quickly when no one stares over her shoulder, and she never shows up to learn she has been locked out. "That's the important part," she says. "I hate wasting time."

I take the hint and have a key to my door made for her, but I am always home on Tuesday mornings.

Another Tuesday, as she comes in my door, when she hears my radio, her head lifts like a startled deer's. "Mozart," she says "Eine Kleine Nacht Musik." She wrestles a dust mop through my door. The long handle is taller than she.

She's wrong. It's one of the Brandenburg Concertos, but right or wrong, that's not the surprise, is it? The short woman who cannot spell *reasonable* confuses Bach with Mozart.

I ask about her children as she moves a dust rag over the bureau top and around Jeanne's framed photo. "Lee D. and Amy," she says.

"Lee D.?"

She pauses to explain. "The *D* is for *Danger*. His Daddy wanted his son to be able to say, 'My middle name is Danger.' Isn't that a hoot?" She smiles that bright full-face smile. "It was the only good thing about the indecent son of a bitch."

I imagine the hellish life Lee D. will have in junior high school. "Amy is a nice name," I say. "What does their father do?"

"I have no idea where Amy's father is. Lee D.'s daddy is in jail."

"I am sorry to hear that," I say.

"Don't be. I put him there." She pauses as if to decide how much I need to know. "Eligible for parole next fall. I don't know what I will do then." She shakes her head with resignation. "Why is there such a thing as parole? Three years should mean three years, right? But now there is talk of rehabilitation and good behavior. That man would not know *good behavior* if it bit him on the ass."

I wonder about the rest, but it is not forthcoming, and I lack the courage to ask. As she mounts the stairs to start her work, she says, "He was a guy with a baseball cap and a mullet," as if that explained something, "and he could name his son *Danger.* And I was that stupid."

Her silence the rest of that morning is like an August day when humidity and sun blossom clouds the color of a bruise. Over our coffee, she is less talkative than usual. Instead, she asks me to tell her more about the big book. Mystery, comedy, or adventure?

I explain that *The Magic Mountain* is none of these things. "It's about ideas," I say.

"What ideas?"

"Complicated ideas."

She stares at me. Raylene knows when she is being patronized. So I take a deep breath. "It's about a young man with no special opinions who goes to a mountaintop sanatorium for tuberculosis. He meets a lot a people who have different ideas about how the world truly works. He tries to decide who might be right and who might be wrong."

"I liked the little bit I read about the baptism. You wonder, what is it like to have family like that? My kids will never know anyone one from their fathers' sides. As for my mother…" she shakes her head. "Gamma raised me, and I am not so sure she was my grandmother. Gamma was a good soul, I'll give her that, but she rode me hard. Hard, I tell you." Raylene stares into her coffee as what I can only call a sardonic grin flits across her lips. "I probably should have listened to her, but when I was fifteen I was a lot smarter than I am now and I did not listen to hardly nobody." Her bright green eyes hold me over the lip of her coffee mug. She is trying not to laugh, waiting like a feral cat. "I also have a brother somewhere in Indiana," she adds, "if he has not moved on. A half-brother."

It is my turn. "My grandchild will never know me," I say. She nods and allows the silence to weigh on us both until I speak again. "He's in Australia. That's a long way to go."

"You should go, anyway," she says.

"I couldn't."

The unasked question hangs in the air. I don't know any answer. Why. I should make the trip while I can still see. I won't, I know.

"Is the book exciting?" she finally asks. "How about the magic?"

It takes me a minute to realize she refers to the title. *The Magic Mountain.* "Not in the way you think. The weather is strange, so the young man loses track of time. Everyone at the hospital is in bad health. So they talk about nothing unless they think it is important. They believe they don't have time."

She stands to rinse her mug. "I would like to read a book like that; it sounds to me like they are dead already, though. I ask you, Bob, who knows how much time they have? Every day is important."

Mann would have liked Raylene.

"I can lend it to you," I say.

That makes her laugh as she rinses her coffee mug clean and places it in my dishwasher. "Oh, no. *I would like to* doesn't mean *I think I can*. Right now, when I make it to the last page of *The Cat in the Hat,* I celebrate. I bet I read that book to Amy and Lee D. a million times. That Dr. Seuss, he has ideas about how the world works, too."

Later that day, I open the bureau drawer beneath Jeanne's wedding picture. From time to time, I like to touch Jeanne's things, and while long ago I gave away all her clothing, I kept her jewelry. Her jewelry is collected in a tin box that once held Danish butter cookies. I suppose I should send the stuff to Australia, but I can't bring myself to part with any of it. I run my fingers through the beads and bracelets when I notice that the cameo cocktail ring I gave Jeanne one Christmas is missing, the profile of a young woman surrounded by a dozen seed pearls, little things, delicate as Jeanne.

I decide I want to be wrong, so I check the jewelry box every Tuesday. As I said, I am prone to imagining things when I cannot see, but I cannot find the ring.

One morning Raylene does not appear. I am annoyed, but then concerned. I pour her undrunk coffee into the sink. She should call. I don't care about the housecleaning, but what if she had a car accident or something? Does she have my number? She must have my number.

I pace through the house like a helpless idiot. Should I go to the Stop 'n' Go and wait to see if she shows up there? If she wants more money, she should ask. I know I am paying her less than I should. I call information. No Raylene Goodheart lives in this town, at least, none with a telephone. Then I remember that Raylene's number is on a stub of green paper that I tore from her advertisement. Fifteen minutes later I locate it in the nightstand drawer under the telephone. I crammed it into my address book like a bookmark.

Her phone rings and rings and rings. I call her three times, every hour. The phone is not disconnected, but it is no cellphone. If it were, I could leave a message. If she is going to use a landline, I will buy her an answering machine. She is in business; she needs an answering machine. She could be losing clients.

I write her number in big bold black Magic Marker, triple ordinary size, under R and under G. RAYLENE GOODHEART. I will be able to see it until I cannot see anything at all. Beneath Jeanne's precise script, my block letters seem peculiar. Here are George and Marilyn Robinson and Harriet Ritter and Jane Rogers and Harold Reichart. Betsy Gallaway and Iris Gordon and Jane and Max Gottlieb. Jeanne knew and liked so many people.

The next day, Wednesday, Raylene shows up at her usual hour. First, I hear her struggling with the lock, and as she backs through the open door opens she calls, "Are you decent?" Lee D. squirms in her arms. I am standing nearby, relieved and happy to see her. She is not ill. She has not left. She pushes the wiggly boy into my hands. "Here," she says and hurries right back out to the truck for the girl, Amy.

Lee D. is cleaner than last I saw him. It has been months. Without a hat, he looks neater, his hair a shock of brownish silk that falls across his forehead. He goes rigid in my grip, but soon relaxes and sucks his thumb, his dark eyes examining me. His head smells shampoo-clean. He is unafraid of the embrace of a stranger.

Raylene returns with the girl and passes Lee D. and me in the doorway. She is a fury of motion, shouting in my kitchen as she runs water into a pail. "I just cannot do it. I am so sorry I did not come yesterday. Lynette is an airhead. An absolute flake. I don't know why I call her 'sister.' She stood me up. She did not call. She did not leave a note. For all I knew, she was dead. Now, would blood do that? I ask you, Bob, would a real sister do that? What am I supposed to do? Blood just don't behave like that. I should have called you, Bob. I know that. I know. But I thought it would just be an hour or so and I'd be here any minute, but no one was available and this morning it's just as bad. Just as bad. I was able to postpone Mrs. Anderson to Saturday morning. She is good that way. Stand still, Amy, help Mommy. Lee D.! You be nice to the nice man. Do you have any cookies? They can watch TV, if that is all right with you. I don't know if I'll be here to finish the job today and you won't have to pay me. Amy, I said 'Stand still.' Lee D. if you need to use the bathroom you speak right up, you hear? No accidents. We are not having accidents today. Now we add ammonia. Yes, I know it smells funny, Amy. It's ammonia. It's supposed to smell funny. I told you the nice man has cable, but I don't know if SpongeBob is on right now. Just tear me a few squares from the paper towels, honey. That's right. I am really so sorry about this Bob, I know you don't care for children. No, I do not mean it that way, Amy. Mr. Bob likes you. Don't cry honey. Please don't cry. I don't know if Mommy could stand it if you cry." She dashes up the stairs with the pail in hand, Amy close behind her. Amy pauses to peer at me through the balustrade. Pressed against two wooden columns, her face is her mother's, etched softer, her skin just as luminous, but hair pure black. "I am Amy and I was born in May," she says. "I am Amy in May." She scoots up the stairs to be with her mother, and calls back, "I start school next year, but I already know how to read." Maybe she wears heavy shoes; maybe she deliberately clomps her feet. Each step is a cannon shot. Boom. Boom. Boom.

"I like children," I shout after her. I am still in my entranceway, frozen to the spot between the living room and the porch.

Lee D. squirms in my arms, serious enough about being uncomfortable that he takes his thumb from his mouth and with two hands pushes against my chest. "Down down down down," he says, but I am not considering anything like that. Jeanne's collection of Hummel figurines on the living room coffee table look too much like toys, and her Wedgewood and Royal Doulton Toby mugs stand on the shelves of the baker's rack at the kitchen door, and while I do not think Lee D. can reach the china, the rack itself has a short leg and is unstable. He could confuse it with a jungle gym or something. So we struggle a little bit until I ask him, "Do you want a cookie?"

I cart him to the kitchen, holding him at the waist as if he were a large, animated loaf of rye bread. I open and shut cabinets, but I already know there's nothing close to a cookie in the pantry. The best I can do is a Ritz Cracker.

Lee D. stuffs a cracker into his pink mouth, I give him another, and shortly we are both covered in a sprinkle of golden crumbs.

"Good cookie?" I ask

Lee D. says. "More."

It has been a while since I had a satisfactory conversation

that called for fewer than five vocabulary words. My finger-tips brush his corn-silk, brown hair from his eyes. I sit on one of the two high stools I have in the breakfast nook, my arm loosely circling his belly as he sits on my lap. I spread four crackers in a square array, then line them up on the counter surface. We try a few configurations. Three in one line, with another on top. Three above and one below. This game makes him laugh, and when I use a cracker to tickle his nose, he laughs more.

What would you give to have Ritz Crackers be a source of pure delight?

One by one, he downs the crackers. I won't dare a glass of milk. The spill, the shattered glass. I need plastic drink-ing glasses for the children, I think. They must sell them at Wal-Mart. Pastels, light green and pink and yellow. Do they still make the spill-proof cups with two handles, weighted bottoms, sealed tops with spouts? It would be just the thing. Sippie cups.

Lee D. squirms uncomfortably, and then suddenly, re-markably, he clambers up to my shoulder, his head goes flat against my chest, and by the soft regularity of his breathing, I am sure he is instantly, happily, blissfully asleep. His clean scalp is right under my nose. It has been a long time since I've felt life and warmth cling to me. So we sit still, Lee D. and I, while upstairs Amy and her mother dust and vacuum and scrub and rinse and wipe and polish.

Age of Marvels? This same filthy kid weeks ago in a shopping cart at the Stop 'n' Go has changed, but not all that much; it must be my vision that changes. I go blind, but I see more every day.

After a time, Raylene puts up the coffee and returns her materials to the garage. Amy has followed her from task to task, silent, dark eyes enormous. When Raylene pulls herself up on the stool opposite mine in the breakfast nook, she says, "Amy wants to know why you have so many books and if she can read one. She wants me to read to her from the one about the magical mountain, if there is a kid version. I told her I did not think there would be, but I also promised I would ask, if she was good. She was. She was good. A big help to her mother."

"How did you help?" I ask. Lee D. breathes softly on my shoulder.

Amy's large eyes blink. Her hands are folded neatly on the table before her, little thumbs intertwined on top. She sits on Raylene's lap. She slowly nods. "I was good. I watched the Cartoon Network the whole time. You have cable TV."

"Yes. I do."

"Do you have the book about magic?"

Raylene takes two sugars with cream. She pours milk for Amy. I take coffee black, but sweet.

Amy's lips are red and round. She speaks slowly and carefully, as if conversation were something new and required special effort. Which, of course, for her, it does. Think of it.

"*The Magic Mountain?*" She nods with great seriousness.

I say, "That's not a book for little girls."

"I'm a big girl. My mommy will read it to me. She reads to me all the time."

Raylene's coffee is hard to explain. It's my Folger's. Same can from the Stop 'n' Go that I always buy. The water is from my tap. Same water I always use. It's my Braun pot. Same cone filters. Nevertheless, when Raylene makes coffee it is more rich and more fragrant than anything I can brew.

"I have a better idea," I say, and gently, so as not to wake Lee D., I stand. He bobs on my shoulder, a pleasant weight.

We'd look like a parade, if anyone watched, as we march to the garage through the door is at the rear of the kitchen and down the three green wooden steps. Since Lee D. fills my arms, I direct Raylene to turn on the light. The wooden scaffold against the rear wall holds a dozen plastic storage boxes.

"It's in one of those," I say. "Look for a label that says, 'Irene.'"

Raylene wrestles two boxes from a rack. Amy stands behind me; there's no real danger, but with kids, you want to be careful. What if something fell? Raylene finds a crate sealed by masking tape on which Jeanne wrote "Irene" in black marker. "Just pull the tape off," I say. It sounds like cloth being ripped, or a zipper. "Open it," I say when Raylene hesitates. "Most of the stuff is junk."

But Irene's abandoned junk is Amy's discovered treasure. There's Mr. Mouse, a blue stuffed animal that went everywhere but Australia. The jewelry box plays Swan Lake and the little ballerina pirouettes in front of the mirror. I forget. All the stuff a kid can have. I forget. I say to Raylene, "If you see any clothes that might fit, take them. If it does not fit now, it may in a year or two." Or three. Or four. Why haven't I donated this crap and taken the tax deductions?

The crate's bottom is lined with books. I tell them to look for *Charlotte's Web*. They find *Little Women*, a hardcover edition with a torn dust jacket and full-page color picture plates, a dozen Birthday Betty outfits that were made in the USA, and a coloring book that has never been touched. But the real discoveries are the copies of *Madeline and Eloise*, appropriate to her age. Amy seizes them along with Mr. Mouse and an untouched coloring book. I have no crayons. I promise Amy a box of Crayolas, and when her mother says nothing, I say,

"The deluxe box. The biggest they have. Fifty colors. A hundred, if they have it. More."

When first I saw the short woman at the Stop 'n' Go, Raylene could deny anything offered to her, but the tiny mother is unable to refuse anything for her children. I see her, new, and I begin to understand her.

"This is a happy box of memories," Raylene says, looking up to me. She kneels on the concrete garage floor beside her daughter.

Amy hugs Mr. Mouse. She holds books against her chest. Raylene tells her how to refold the top panels of the plastic storage container. "There'll be more to find another day," she says. They push the box back against the wall on the floor. The space above the shelf where the box had been looks terribly empty.

Lee D. stirs and I hand him to his mother. The parade reforms; we march back to the house. In the living room, Raylene softly reads to Amy.

> *In an old house in Paris,*
> *That was covered with vines*
> *Lived twelve little girls,*
> *In two straight lines.*

"What's a *pendix*?" Amy asks later as Raylene turns the pages. Lee D. lies on his back beside me on the sofa, his dark eyes wide and open, soothed by the lilting music of his mother's voice. He twirls his hair as he drifts in and out of sleep, his sneakers against my thigh.

"She needs an operation," Raylene says.

Where was Raylene educated? I wonder, my tiny housekeeper who knows Mozart, hungers for Thomas Mann, who cannot be bought for the price of Animal Crackers?

Lee D. fully awakens just as Amy sinks into sleep. This is the shape of Raylene's life, I realize. When one sleeps, the other awakes.

That's too hard, I think. Too hard for the short woman.

"There were five years between our children," I say.

"That's nice timing," Raylene says ruefully as she gathers up what she must. I carry a pail with a mop in it to the big red truck. First, she buckles the sleeping Amy into her seat. Then Lee D., who resists only a little. She climbs behind the wheel, starts the engine, and says, "I'll be here my usual time next week, if that is all right. This is usually library day."

"You didn't have to be here today."

"The hell I did not," she says. "You keep saying stuff like that, Bob, but I don't do nothing I don't have to do. Or choose. You must have noticed that by now."

I have, I tell her. With one foot on the running board, talking through her truck window, I explain my theory of how the Stop 'n' Go is the paradigm of life. "We all start with the same empty cart," I say. "You might have bad luck and draw a cart with a sticky wheel, but once it is your cart, it is your cart for as long as you want. You can walk any path you want through the store. No one cares what route you take. You can explore any aisles in any order. You can omit whole aisles; you can stroll up and own the same aisle two or three times. Haven't you ever gone down an aisle a second or third time and spied things you did not notice before? We fill our carts as we see fit, and we live with what we take."

Burdened by babies and weary from work, Raylene listens to my metaphysics. She allows me to finish, but as I utter each sentence more pretentious than the last, I can see her incredulity tempered only by politeness. Jeanne had a facial expression like that. I'd ramble on, and the more I prattled on, the more her face deflated me.

I leave out the part about how some of us persist in pushing sticky wheels despite the fact that we are free to turn in our carts at any time, when Raylene says, "Bob, are we going to be friends?"

I tell her I think we already are.

She nods, pleased. "Bob, you are maybe the smartest man I will ever know, but Bob, the Stop 'n' Go ain't nothing but a damned grocery store."

I hear her laughing as she pulls away, and the sound makes me smile.

I don't soon see the children again, but Raylene arrives as ever on the next Tuesday and begins her chores by saying, "Amy says 'Hey.'" Raylene reports that Amy can already read Madeline herself. She likes the watercolors of Paris.

"Tell her the crayons are here," I say. When did they change the names of all the colors?

On another Tuesday, Raylene discovers a carrot cake muffin in my pantry. After her chores, and after asking my permission, she slices it in half as if it were a rare delicacy. Muffins become a regular part of our time together. We take the occasional flyer on banana nut or poppy seed, but carrot cake remains our first true love. Our muffin ceremony consists of Raylene swearing she will only have half, and then breaking down to eat the second half despite herself. It not-so-incidentally means she lingers thirty minutes more with me, so every Monday I make certain to buy four muffins at the Stop 'n' Go.

Raylene becomes harried and frustrated; word of mouth has made her clientele more numerous than she can handle.

She reschedules me to Tuesday afternoons instead of mornings because she needs the morning for a house on Elm in Pinehurst. She keeps Wednesday afternoons redlined. That is inviolable library time for Lee D. and Amy. Some of her first clients become insulted when they recommend her to their friends or neighbors and Raylene has to say, "No." She could not work for a Mrs. Williamson, but just two days later Mrs. Freeman's husband, Arthur, accepted the transfer to the Milwaukee office. With her schedule opening up, Raylene called Mrs. Williamson back, "But by then, she'd hired someone else."

"What did you tell her?"

"That if it didn't work out, to be sure to call me. But she won't, Bob. That woman did not hire nobody else. Her pride was hurt when I turned her down. People get weird when they come to housework. Weird, Bob, weird." Raylene receives special requests, too. Anniversaries. Birthday parties. There was a first-communion party thrown by an Italian woman who did not want to be a regular but just wanted one day of help. "But I was not about to wear that uniform she wanted to rent. Where do folks get such airs?"

More and more of her clientele is from west of Grand Street and east of the river north of the bend, which means big Queen Anne homes with lots of paneled woodwork and lots of old money. She is becoming frazzled and tired, but the income is too good. "I need to learn how to say *No*," Raylene says.

"I disagree," I say. "You need to hire help."

She puts down her mug with a bang and stares at me as if I had slithered down the gangway of a flying saucer. "Well, now I know you are a crazy old man," she says. I can tell by how she says it that the idea is one she came to herself, but has no idea how to go forward. She is probably frightened of the prospect.

So I give her the short version of the three-week university workshop about entrepreneurship. Her business has attained critical mass: her clientele is self-sustaining and self-renewing on the demand side, but Raylene is up against the limits of her capacity to match demand with supply. "You are fresh out of labor," I say, "unless you are willing to quit going to the library or want to work on weekends."

She shakes her head.

I explain that the crucial issue for expansion of a service business is training. Hardee's is a pit and Starbucks thrives because Starbucks learned the trick of teaching people to make a double decaf latte or a skim milk double-shot espresso while burger places will let any acne-ridden high school flunky flip beef. Every business has its finesse. Donut makers go to Donut College. So I say, "Can you train other women to do what you do?"

"There's nothing to teach," Raylene laughs. "You start on the left, go around the room, and apply elbow grease. In a big room, don't try to clean more than you can reach with two steps; you have to sort of divide the room up in your head." In this light in the breakfast nook, I see how clear green here eyes can be.

"If it were that easy, then everyone would be cleaning houses. Why do you think all the women who are making demands on your time aren't searching for other cleaning services?"

She listens as I tell her how she might plan, and as I do her eyes first widen and then narrow as I answer each of her doubts and with a new possibility. Geoff's room upstairs can become an office. All we'll need is a phone, a desk, and a filing cabinet. New employees must first go out with Raylene to watch and learn, not to mention build confidence in the client. Eventually, the new employee can be sent out alone. "But only after I say OK," Raylene interrupts me.

"The chief asset of a service business is your reputation. You have to guard it," I agree, and the little woman nods.

"And that's why no one but me holds the keys to the houses," she says. "After a while, I just open the lock and let them in. That's right, isn't it, Bob? Think of it. We might be doing three or four houses at the same time."

I think of Jeanne's cameo ring, but instead I ask, "What's your schedule now?"

"One house in the morning and one house in the afternoon, if neither is too big. What kills me is when they are far apart. There is no time for lunch when I have to haul my bony ass across town. I suppose with enough business, I can make better schedules," she says, and five minutes after saying that Raylene is asking me if it might be better to send three girls to a single address all at once. "Maybe as a team they can handle four or five houses in a day. One of them would have to be in charge. Like a team captain."

Logistics and deployment? Piece of cake. Raylene is quicker than any student in my university course has ever been. Don't explain excess value-add or hierarchical organizational structures to Raylene—she is way ahead of you. She calls Lynette to say she will be late.

Our customary thirty-minute coffee stretches to three hours. Raylene brews an unprecedented second pot and picks the walnuts from the top of a second muffin without any pretense of slicing it. She can only hire women with cars, she can see that. She likes the notion that we ask them to buy their own brushes, rags, cleaners and such, but she is willing to lend any new employee whatever money she needs to get started. "That way, they already like us for helping them out," she says, rolls her eyes, and adds, "And they pay us back, guaranteed. It's so sweet. We just deduct it from their first pay. It's not like a loan." I wonder how soon she can get the job as chair of the university Business Department. Maybe dean of the College.

Her good soul wants to supply free daycare for employees, but I say that so kind an idea has to wait because what it will cost in insurance. She says, "Insurance?" and I explain how she cannot go forward without it. "Someone, sometime, someplace is going to break a bowl or ruin a carpet, and you can expect people will expect you to pay for it." She chews her lip at this. "Look, it's better to pay a few dollars to an insurance company than it is to go bankrupt because someone dumps bleach on an Afghan rug. You carry insurance on the truck, don't you?"

"Well, that's the law."

"Now you know why it is the law."

Maybe it is the extra caffeine, but the little woman becomes animated. I've seen this a few times with students, not many, but it always makes the small hairs on the back of my neck stand on end. Raylene's vaguest dreams are coalescing into a graspable vision.

We talk about limited liability partnerships and incorporation; we talk about social security taxes, and when she looks a little doubtful and a little fearful about the enormity of what we are discussing, I say, "Why don't you just let me take care of it?"

"You've got to explain, though, Bob. I won't go ahead with anything that I do not understand. I could not allow that."

I agree, and so without much conversation we are partners. I propose a sixty-forty split in her favor of all revenues
earned by employees after expenses, but she will keep all
monies earned by her own labor, just as it has always been.

She chews her lip and shifts her weight on my breakfast
nook stool. Her feet swing several inches from the floor. I
suspect this deal will earn me not so much as a nickel until
we have employees working 200 hours per week, and I suspect that will never happen, but I why would I care about the
money? She says, "Fifty-fifty or nothing," and I laugh.

It will be a classic partnership. Our skills complement
each other. From synergies spring profit. Raylene may be able
to end her food-stamp life and never again dump her purse in
search of nickels.

She leaps to her feet. For a moment, I think she will spit
into her palm before she ceremonially pumps my arm with
two hard handshakes. "There," she says. "It's a deal."

"I'll have to file papers," I say. "You'll need to sign
them."

She sags as if I have punched her. "I can't have that," she
says.

"It's ordinary business," I say. "It protects us both."

She weighs this new part of the proposition. "I can't have
that," she repeats. "I guess we are busted."

"What are you talking about?" I ask.

Her fist pats her thigh. "Could we just make it your business? Keep my name out of it?"

"We could, but you'd have to be a silent partner."

"I could not be silent."

"It's just an expression."

"Well, all right then. Keep my name out of it. All the
papers in your name and we are partners on a handshake."

Our business plan is settled. I walk her to the door. "What do you think of *Raylene's Cleaning*," I say.

She freezes with her hand on the doorknob, and when she turns to me, even a blind man can see the panic in her face. I am having an attack of floaters—too much coffee. Dark dots occlude the center of my vision. Sometimes I think going blind at a single stroke would be easier. A bolt of lightning from God would suit me more than having my sight bleed away, the constant reminder of oncoming perpetual night.

"That's no way to keep my name out of it, Bob" she says. "We can't call it that. Not that."

"You've got a reputation…" I am about to start my lecture on branding and goodwill.

"No, Bob. No." I keep my mouth shut. "It's not me. It's James. Lee D.'s father. James Boncoeur. Don't ever call him *Jimmy*. He hates *Jimmy*. James will come looking for me. I know he will. It's just a matter of time. Nothing stops James if he has a mind. He will. James is a goddam force of nature. When he gets out, he will come looking. I was careful when I came here, but James has his ways. Someone always knows someone who always knows someone and that person knows me. So it is just a matter of time. We can't call the business anything with *Raylene*. It will cut the time it takes him to find me. My life is permanently temporary."

I ask if a restraining order will be a condition of his parole, and Raylene says, "You may know about checkbooks and taxes, but where I come from a restraining order ain't nothing but a PDC." She sees my puzzled expression. "Pre-death certificate."

As if to persuade me of the seriousness of the situation, she turns, bends, and pulls her shirt up. She arches like a cat's back. Raylene wears no bra this day. The skin of her back is luminous as ever. I can make out the knuckles of her spine, where her ribs push at her skin, and I can see above the crowned two-headed falcon tattooed on her back a circle of six angry red scars, each the size of a dime, the circle four inches in diameter, scars made with a cigarette. That much is plain.

"That's not the worst," she says, as she tucks her shirt into her pants, her back still to me. "It's Amy he wanted."

As she hurries down the steps and along my flagstone walk, she calls back to me, "You think of a name, Bob. Think of a name." The red truck roars into life. She pops the clutch, the rear wheels grab the street, and I think I hear her shout, "But keep my name out of it."

I hear her drive away.

The trees are leafy in May. Amy's birthday must be soon. Amy in May. I need to know the date because if she is starting school in September, I want to buy her a fancy notebook. Maybe a backpack. The wind stirs the trees. There's just enough wind to make that leafy sound. The clear blue sky is dotted by a few clouds, huge and white; it's a child's picture book sky. I can look at the sky and see it as it is...plain as day.

I sit a long while on my cement steps, the village idiot gazing up at Heaven. My neighbor waves to me as he walks across his lawn. I wave back at him. I think he nods, but I can't see until he is close. He wears boxy brown shoes and an undone yellow necktie. His name is Smith or Johnson or Jones. Something ordinary. He is an ordinary guy who in an ordinary way comes across my driveway to me. He wipes his palms on his slacks before he shakes my hand. He tells me that in the coming weeks—he's not sure when they will start, contractors being what they are—a crew of landscaping guys will be working on his front lawn. How's that for ordinary? "You may want to pull further into the driveway," he says. "I'll be sure they keep it clear, but what with trimming the trees and what all to make space for a small pine, you may want to pull your car all the way in. Keep it safe from woodchips or whatever." He points at the big oak set in the sidewalk between our places. Its roots buckle the pavement. It must be four or five feet around, an ordinary tree.

I thank him for the warning. We shake hands, and he says something ordinary about how we men have to do things to keep wives happy, how I must know how it is, and we share a masculine chuckle at the futility of dissuading women from redecorating, or landscaping, or some other fool project. "I just wanted to give you the 'head's up,'" he says, and adds, "Likely not until fall. They want the sap receding." As he turns to go, as if it were an afterthought he turns back to me and says, "There's a zoning hearing. I need a variance." I tell him I can't imagine that will be a problem. "In a few years, the tree might cast shade on your property," he says. "I want you to know it all in advance." I thank him again as he nods affirmation and in his ordinary, decent way ambles back to his front door. He has a wife and teenage children, I think. Two or three. I've never really noticed. It's not something I've needed to see.

He waves to me from his front steps, identical to mine, and as his screen door bangs shut, I think how ordinary is a good thing.

Those burn marks must have been deep to have never fully healed, made by more than a touch, and then I realize that since they are in a near-perfect circle, all six of them, the cigarette had to have been applied by someone who was being deliberate and could take his time. I spread my fingers. They were closer together than that, and I see how James must have restrained her while he did his work. Did he hold her or tie her?

It is much too horrible beneath the perfect blue sky and white clouds on this spring day to think about those details, but that's the problem with a practiced imagination; visions come, unbidden.

My relentless imagination runs mind-movies all that night.

By summer's end, Amy and Lee D. call me "Mr. Bob." The Traveling Goodheart Circus arrives at my house about once a week, sometimes more. Amy discovers treasure after treasure among Irene's castoffs; Lee D. in a year or two may find the same in the crates labeled "Geoffrey." I plan a tetherball court on the backyard. Dig a hole, plant a pole, anchor it with cement. Even a blind man can manage that.

At the mall, I buy a folding playpen, though Raylene tells me he should be outgrowing such devices. Lee D., however, adores his private space in the living room. Raylene makes no other comment, which I have come to understand is as close as she allows herself to expressing satisfaction.

Best Cleaners grows. We employ Amber, Heather and Wendy, steady, good women who work well without strong supervision. Happy to have jobs, they are honest and become loyal. Where did Raylene find such women? I wonder, but Raylene says, "Good people are all over the place, Bob. All they require is a chance."

Establishing Heather with a set of regulars requires more effort than it should, but I make the phone calls to clients that need to hear a man's authoritative voice. Heather is black, and in this enlightened corner of the world where everyone gives lip service to hearty endorsements against racism, when a black woman draws near the silverware, they still require re-assurances. Heather, who has traveled this road many times, just says, "Thanks, Mr. Bob," and goes about her tasks. She is, by the way, faster at her work than even Raylene.

But early in July, we have to let Enid, a fourth girl, go. We hire Enid in the same way we hire everyone else, though I have no idea what that is. Enid fails to show up three times in two weeks, and after our pointed requests nevertheless seems incapable of making a phone call to alert us. One thing or another disrupts her life, her no-good husband, her boy, her car, her cramps, her cell phone's dead battery. "Maybe she is running hard luck," I say, but Raylene snaps, "Cut her loose," and that is the end of the conversation between Best Cleaners' senior partners. I slip Enid a $50 bill from my own pocket when I fire her. She thanks me, folds the bill into a neat square, and slips it into her jeans. She has been at this crossroads before, I realize.

None of the women choose to work more than four days each week. These are mothers of young children. They need a few dollars and flexible hours. Raylene reserves her Wednesdays for the library, and while I do not know the details of the others' lives, I am sure they do something similar with their free weekday. They all want to be home by 3:30 P.M. when their kids arrive from school. In some businesses, that seems a liability; we take it to be the sign of a responsible person. I often worked at the office until 6:00 or 7:00 in the evening, later in tax season. What good did it do me?

In summer, they make child-care arrangements. I gather that all over town there are ad hoc summer cooperative day-care centers—probably unlicensed, illegal, and therefore affordable.

In July's high heat, the girls dress lightly, and they are careless about themselves in front of me. They scratch when they itch. They work bra-less for comfort's sake, and they wear thin cotton shirts. Housecleaning is no act of haute couture. Why not relax? The old man is invisible, anyway. Wendy and Amber have the same tattoo as Raylene. The same, but different. I make no apology for seeing what I see; I am sixty-two, I say and do nothing to make them uncomfortable, and if the girls notice my looking, they either do not mind or, perhaps, they enjoy my appreciation. I don't stare. With my eyes, anything at the center of my vision soon disappears.

We redefine a "good client" as someone who leaves the air-conditioning on for the cleaning girl. Some do; most don't. At thirty, Amber is oldest, her legs skinny and long. Her hair is short as mine. Wendy smiles easily and laughs too hard, and Heather is always first to appear in the morning, drinking more coffee than anyone else, black with two sugars. Like me.

Best Cleaners grows to have about thirty steady clients. Some come and go, but counting one-timers on average we do seventy addresses each month at an average of $100 each visit. The house keys hang on a pegboard in Geoff's room. The pegboard was Raylene's idea, the product of her frustration of trying to find a set of keys in a drawer. She divided the board into five columns, Monday through Friday, with yellow electrical tape, and with blue tape she lined four rows, one for each week of the month. Our pegboard calendar reveals at a glance what is what. Each set of keys is on a small chain attached to a small cardboard disk with the first initial of the employee who generally does the work. The address is on a bit of masking tape beneath the keys. When the girls have their emergencies—and they do—they cover each other. They pool their tips; no one squabbles over generous clients.

From time to time, Raylene drops in on the girls at work, as much to assist as to maintain quality control. The girls—which is what Raylene insists on calling them, so I develop the habit, too—enjoy her company. We pay by the hour after gauging how long a job should take, but we estimate on the generous side and embrace the point of view that a job done is a job done. That means an employee can finish early, garner the same paycheck, and skedaddle. So who'd resent a boss who grabs a wet mop to help?

When Wendy's boy comes down with chickenpox, the girls cover for her for three days. She does not miss a dollar. When she returns she cries a little as she says "Thanks," and when Heather's mother takes ill, Wendy can't do enough overtime for her.

One morning, as I walk past them on my way from the office upstairs to the kitchen, they stop talking. When I bend to take milk from the refrigerator, they burst into laughter. My T-shirt? My shorts? I will never know about what is funny, but the sound is pleasant, and when later I ask Raylene what that was about she says, "Never you mind, Bob. Girl-talk."

I keep the books on a laptop spreadsheet, but by August I have to increase the font. When I drive, I take care of everything on my left while God protects my right. At the Stop 'n' Go, I park far away from the other cars. A little extra walking is a good thing, right? I park on the white lines. If you've been cursing the old fart who takes up two spaces, that old fart would be me.

And one hot afternoon when the air in the house is superheated and dry as dust, I open Jeanne's drawer and the jewelry box. The missing cameo ring sits on top of everything else.

Dust motes float in the ray of sunlight that slices through the space where the drapes meet. It is funny, the things I can see and the things I cannot. If the ring was not there before, now it is. If the jewelry was pawned, it has been redeemed.

In August, when the air is heavy with water sucked from the black earth, when the corn outside town stands head high, a day when tornadoes may be breeding somewhere as the thunder boomers mount and grow dark, Raylene finishes early and I ask her to stay with me for a rundown on how we are doing. She stands in front of the office fan and airs her armpits, flapping her elbows like a chicken. I tell her that our clients are paying on time. They are regular, good customers who like us. They enclose thank you notes with the checks, a good sign. If Raylene wants, we can manage one more employee. She shakes her head.

"One more thing," I say. I hand Raylene her first dividend check.

"This is a thousand dollars," she says, amazed. Her voice is hushed. "Are you playing with me, Bob, you old rascal? A thousand dollars? Really?" She does a little dance that makes me laugh.

I say, "It could have been more." I can see her look of amazement. "I have held some back for the business. Emergencies. Bills. Things like that. If you need to draw, let me know. We have money in the bank."

The bank account has our two names on it. That required a long conversation and two days before I could persuade her to sign the bank form, and she did so only after I asked what would happen to her money if I died, and only after I assured her no one but the government can force the bank to give up her name and address. A silent partner can be silent only so long.

She shakes her head and sits on the wooden captain's chair that Geoffrey used to study in when he was a high school student. Her reality is changing. Who she is. What she does. Who she thinks she is. I look at the little women, her red hair and blue kerchief, her bangs aflutter in the fan's breeze, her sponge yellow halter, her jeans shorts, her bare feet in open-toe, blue, high-heel sneakers, and her scarlet toenail polish. She holds the check with two hands. Her feet don't reach the floor. It is not the air-conditioning that gives me goose bumps.

"You took the same?" Raylene asks suddenly.

"Of course," I lie.

"Damn, Bob. Damn." She jumps to her feet again and holds the check held out at arm's length in her two hands before her. "This is a fine thing," Raylene says. "A fine, fine thing."

That day when Raylene leaves me, at the door she tiptoes to kiss my cheek and asks, "Bob, isn't it time you told me what is wrong with your eyes?"

"What makes you think I have eye trouble?"

She has noticed my head bobbles as if I cannot keep her in focus when I look at her, and she tells me that I do not seem to look directly at her but off to one side or the other, but Raylene tells me that the giveaway is the magnifying glass on the dining room table beside my bookstand. "That wasn't there when I first met you."

I explain macular degeneration to Raylene, as though it has any explanation that is sensible. I try to sound casual about it, as if it was a natural part of growing old, which is what my doctor wants me to believe. The brochure from my ophthal-mologist shows a cheerful looking woman on the cover. She is smiling; perpetual night is a mere inconvenience, no worse than nail fungus. I do not tell Raylene the pact I have made with myself for when I cannot see at all. I will do what I have to do. God will be my judge.

"That is too hard," she says. She abruptly spins on her heel and walks away across my lawn to her truck on the street, but then she quickly comes back up the walk. "Should you drive?" she asks.

"I am all right, so far." Her hands are deep in her back pockets and she peers at the floor near her feet, her posture whenever talk becomes serious. She chews her lip. I know her tics. She waits for me to speak, and I say, "I promise I will tell you when I cannot drive."

She nods. "All right, then. But I will read to you," she says. "You can't read with no magnifying glass."

"It's not so bad," I say, but she will hear nothing more about it.

So Raylene makes time to read to me near every day for near thirty minutes at the day's end. Sometimes she picks up the kids before she arrives. She juggles her schedule to move my cleaning day to Wednesday mornings. Some days she brings the children so that after lunch they can make faster time to the library. They also visit me on some Saturdays.

Amy comes to rely on my cable television. Lee D. knows where I keep his cookies. He prefers Animal Crackers but will indeed accept Ritz if I am out of stock.

One day in August, the sirens wail when a twister snakes from the sky somewhere nearby, and shortly after the all-clear sounds, Raylene telephones.

"You all right?" she asks.

"I'm just fine," I say. "You?"

"We're sitting pretty," the little mother says, and after another minute or two of small talk we hang up.

In the cooling evening, I sit on my cement front steps.

Come Labor Day, as I make my way through Register 4 with my green leafy vegetables, Animal Crackers for Lee D., carrot-cake muffins for Raylene and me, and what turns out to be five sacks of groceries filled with who knows what, none other than Beth Anne says, "How are you?"

I have achieved visibility. I ask how her obvious pregnancy is treating her, and she rolls her eyes. She tells me, "I call you *Mr. Animal Crackers* and *Carrot Cake Muffin*." She smiles and touches the piercing in her eyebrow. "You must like Animal Crackers a lot." I confess that I do, and she waves to me as I exit through the electric eye door.

As I drive home, the lane markers snake before my drusen-warped vision, I see the splendid world we inhabit. At the edge of town, cornfields stretch as far as anyone can see. A west wind carries the smell of growth and renewal, the rich smell of fecund life springing from black earth. If you drive just a little farther into dairy country, you are among barns, Holsteins and silos set like toys on rolling green hills. The trees in my neighborhood, oak and spruce, full and green, lower their arms to the ground, but with university students newly returned to town, the sense of fall is in the air. In a matter of weeks, the leaves will turn crimson and orange and yellow and then brown.

I am at my car's open trunk retrieving my groceries when I notice the man sitting in the center of my three cement front steps. You can't go around him, by him, or over him. He drops a cigarette between his knees and crushes it with his black boot as he stands to greet me at my own door. "You'd be Mr. Evans?" he says and tips his Expos baseball cap and runs a hand back over his scalp. He scoops a grocery package from my arms. He takes it from me easily.

"Can I help you?" I say.

He opens my unlocked house door, and when I do not invite him in, he places the grocery sack on the porch. "Maybe. Maybe you can help. You see, sir, I am looking for someone," he says. "My wife, actually. Raylene Boncoeur. Well, she was my wife, once." He walks beside me back to my car. There's an unfamiliar Dodge pickup parked two doors down, the same diesel model as Raylene's, but black, and I am wondering how fast I can get to the baseball bat when he says, "James Boncoeur," and puts out his hand. "She may not be calling herself that, anymore. 'Boncoeur,' I mean. She might be calling herself Raylene Shaughnessy." I take his outstretched hand. His grip is gentle, even respectful. Under the black stubble on his throat, I see the tattooed cross on his neck set well above his shirt collar. I can't tell if the cross is wavy from my sight of if it is just amateurish work, maybe self-inflicted. The cross' arms aren't crooked enough to be a swastika; I can see that even with my sad old eyes. "Shaughnessy was her name when we met? Her people are Scottish and something else I cannot recall. But mostly Aryan?" He makes statements that sound like questions. "She's a red-headed gal."

"Why would I know her?"

"She's got two children with her, sir. One of them is my boy? I'd like to see him? You can understand that, I am sure?" He lifts two sacks of groceries and I take the last one as he reaches up to close my car trunk. "I am on my way north tomorrow, so this is a long shot. There's a job waiting for me up in Marquette? An interview, anyways. Crew of a lake ship. But I do want to see my boy, if I can, before I ship out? You can understand that." He chatters on about the opportunities in the Upper Peninsula, a place where a white man can still work with his hands and make a respectable living, provided he has regular habits. "It's close to my people," he says. "I am a white American, but from Canadian stock. *Boncoeur.* That's French. Means *good heart.* They speak French in parts of Canada. Did you know that?"

"Is that a fact?" I say.

As if we are old friends, we walk to the house. He asks me if I have something wrong with my vision, and I tell him that I do. "I thought for a minute you were giving me the evil eye," he says. "I am sorry for your trouble. No offense."

As we reach the steps again, my neighbor, the ordinary man, shouts a greeting and scoots over to tell me that the landscaping will begin the very next day. "They figure four weeks, but I am betting more." He describes the flagstone walk, the hedges, the flowerbed, and the new pine tree he expects will grow so high it will blot out the sun.

"James Boncoeur," James Boncoeur says, wiggling his fingers, unable to extend his hand to my neighbor with dropping the groceries clutched to his chest. "That new tree will look fine come Christmas."

"Pleased to meet you," my neighbor says. "Art Jones."

We hear more about Art Jones' plans. I have not exchanged this many words with Jones in fifteen years. We are three men of the world, we are, one blind old man without the strength to hold onto his groceries, one ordinary man with an ordinary name who is planting a tree, and one sadistic jailbird just out and intent on God alone knows what.

When Art Jones heads back, James Boncoeur says to me, "Nice fella," and without waiting for an invitation, this time he heads across my modest enclosed porch and through the front door and through my living room toward the kitchen as though we are old friends. He passes Lee D.'s folded playpen as if it were not there, and he places the grocery sacks on my breakfast nook table.

"See, now," he says, "My Raylene moves around some, and she sometimes works as a housecleaner. I heard you run a business like that." He shakes his head and smiles about how all he had to do was go to the library and on a computer there type into Google the telephone number a nice lady gave him. Google supplies a reverse telephone book, and the lady lived on the east side of the river, a better neighborhood. He just went door to door. "Ain't technology wonderful?" he says, and lowers his eyes when he adds, "All those young mothers needing work. You must get plenty, you old dog." He lightly punches my bicep. James and I are old buddies. "You haven't seen a short red-headed woman? Maybe she dyed her hair? Maybe you didn't hire her, but she applied? This is Best Cleaners, am I right? Oh, you'd remember Raylene if you met her. She's a pistol."

I thank him for his help with the packages and ask him to wait while I go upstairs. "I'll check my records," I say. He puts his hands in the back pockets of his jeans the same way Raylene does, and I leave him standing there, just a good old boy in jeans with a Montreal Expos baseball cap, a black Dodge truck, a haircut called a mullet, and the heart of a Gestapo interrogator. His hair is dyed a bright, unnatural yellow on the sides.

Upstairs, I find the bat. The heft feels fine. It's not three foot long, a kid's baseball bat, actually. I smack it into my left palm. It will do. Geoff played second base and was awful at the game. Could not judge a fly ball with a compass and an astrolabe. But his bat will do. I take a cut at the air; the swing pains my shoulder.

I flush the toilet so James will know why I have delayed. I want him off guard, but I have no plan. I finally understand why homeless men kill each other over trifles. When you have little, you defend it ferociously.

Since my neighbor saw James, an affable man in a jeans jacket with his arms full of my groceries, I will have to explain that the stranger who broke in intent on doing me harm terrorized me. After years of use, the stairs creak from weight in their centers, so I move to the edge where the old wood make less sound. They will ask how I got the drop on him. You retrieved a baseball bat? How did you manage that, Mr. Evans? I want to come down on him from behind, but that is chancy. I put the bat in my left hand and grip the smooth handrail with my right. How will I get behind him? If I don't brain him with the first blow, he'll have me. He's young; he's strong; he's quick. I am old and going blind, but not frail. Not yet. The trick is to swing low across his legs, get lucky, hit a knee, and only then his head.

I rush the kitchen from the base of the stairs. I swing. The bat meets only air.

James is gone.

My groceries are neatly set out on the table, canned goods beside fresh produce. The brown paper bags are neatly folded on the high stool. The faint stench of tobacco lingers.

I open the door to the garage and tiptoe down the wooden steps, and then I slap the wall plate that is the electric garage door opener. I haven't worked the garage door in years. The pulleys and rusted springs creak as the door rises. The last of the day's light floods in under the rising door. Under a blue plastic tarp at the edge of my narrow driveway are two bags of cement mix, the future anchor to Lee D's and Amy's tetherball court. I hold the bat rigid against my leg. I slowly walk up the narrow driveway. I stop at the front of my car.

James' black truck is gone from the street.

I lift his cigarette butt from my front walk and find three others. Marlboros, I think. He must have waited a long while. Where has he gone? Will he be back? I hear cicadas. Evening comes earlier this time of the year, though it is still warm.

I make a selfish, criminally self-serving wager with God, cheap for me, but dear for Raylene. I gamble that James spoke truth and is hurrying to the Upper Peninsula.

God forgive me, I say nothing to the short woman.

I endure a bad week, but my bet seems a winner. I pray that James Boncoeur joins the crew of a lake vessel, and when I hum "The Wreck of the Edmund Fitzgerald" I pray that the witch of November comes early.

Amy's class performs a Columbus Day recital. They sing patriotic songs and Native American songs; because we are in this part of the world they enact a scene that suggests a regional orthodoxy, that the Vikings arrived on North American shores before other Europeans. Since Raylene cannot attend because she has two houses to do that day, and since Amber and Heather are fully booked, and since Wendy has taken some overtime to work after someone's 50th anniversary party, I stand in as Amy's consolation prize. I never had the patience for these things when Geoffrey and Irene were children. A teacher calls me *grandfather*, but I do not correct her. She is right. I am a grandfather, just not Amy's.

Amy wears a white shirt and pink jeans, nothing special. All the kids look clean and well maintained, which if you ask me is plenty these days. They sing with their hands clasped behind their backs, their mouths perfect little circles and their eyes the same. But the school! The school is a charmless four-story pile of red brick that could be mistaken for a power station or a prison. The ceiling in the auditorium flakes with water damage.

Would Raylene move in with me? All I know is that she lives across the river near the railroad. It can't be much of a neighborhood; nothing over there is. I have space enough. Too much. Should James Boncoeur return, he will come straight here, so I am raising the stakes of my wager with God, but the little mother will risk anything for her children, and the school near my house is the best in town; at least it used to be.

When Wendy is late for work two days running, Raylene guesses she has morning sickness, and sure enough Wendy shares her news with the entire crew of Best Cleaners at the next morning shape-up. Heather takes away her coffee and fills a glass with milk, and Raylene says, "Well, that's wonderful, Wendy," and hugs her. "You just tell us what you can or can't do. You need time, you tell us. Will that be all right?" Wendy is a big woman. Nordic maybe, with boat hips and shoulders. She must weigh twice what Raylene does.

Raylene creates our maternity policy on the fly. She comes to this stroke of managerial brilliance in front of the other two girls, and I tell you the effect is electrifying. It's not lost on me that more and more she talks about Best Cleaners as "us," a joint enterprise that includes our employees. In all my years at the doll company I never saw anything like it. These women's only jobs have been exercises in mistrust, a presumption that they will do as little as possible for the most they can get, but here is Raylene, unmistakably in charge, but choosing to abandon power in favor of cultivating loyalty with kindness. How will Raylene look on the cover of Forbes?

One evening, Raylene and I sit on the cement steps at my front door. The children have just fallen asleep, and she is reluctant to awaken them to drive home. It is not the first time she will spend the night, sharing Amy's bed. The fall night grows chilled quickly. We wear sweaters, but cold still clutches at my ribs. Stars hard as pins burn in a cloudless night. I think I see fireflies, but there are no fireflies at this time of the year. The cells in my eyes discharge a final electrical impulse as they die, starved of blood. Or maybe the flashes are my imagination. What I can't see, I imagine. Like faith.

Raylene's whisper suddenly percolates from the darkness. "I've done bad in my time, Bob." I can hardly see her shape in the dim light. Her presence is a feeling, more than a testimony of vision. Our voices float.

I say nothing; she repeats her confession.

"What of it?" I say. "Who hasn't?"

"You're a kind man, Bob, so you don't imagine the bad people can do. You just always trusted me, haven't you?"

"That's true," I say, and think of the cameo ring, the jewelry taken and then restored.

"See now, Bob, that's plain foolishness. You don't know what I am capable of. I've done things that make me ashamed. Don't you ever suspicion me? Just a little?"

"Never," I lie.

"I've done terrible things, Bob. Terrible."

The moon is a silver cup in heaven's ink-black dome. Raylene touches the back of my hand with her fingertips, as intimate a gesture as she knows, and then, to join her children at my TV before they leave, she slips through the dark open door, gently shutting it behind her.

My random act of kindness to the little mother in the checkout aisle has paid a high dividend. On that day, she told me that she could not be bought cheap.

She never said she could not be bought.

I cross my legs, uncross them, cross them at the ankles, and lean my head back against the screen door. Was Raylene ever sold? If so, what of it? Who doesn't have a past? We live in the present. Even a blind man can see that.

The door to cracks open. She is barefoot. She's quiet until she says, "Do you want me to read to you tonight?"

"Not tonight." We're working our way through *Oliver Twist*. Amy likes the parts with Fagin. Her head emerges. I turn to look in her direction, but I can't really see her, so I face the street more. "Bob," she says, "Tell me true. Why ain't you never tried nothing funny with me?"

"I don't think of you that way," I lie.

I can feel her breathing not two feet behind me. "You are so full of shit," she says, and the door shuts with finality.

I fix on the idea of hosting Thanksgiving dinner for Raylene and the children, but the idea takes on life and grows. Why not all of our employees? all their kids, their husbands if they have them, their boyfriends, anyone they really want? Why not? What else is money for? Best Cleaners has much to be thankful for. After that dinner, I will offer Raylene and the children my home.

One overcast afternoon when the clouds have been lead all day, after I've accomplished my routines, opened the mail, deposited checks, and made a few spot-check calls to keep customers happy, I scoot over to the Stop 'n' Go. I like to shop earlier now that the light of day scatters by five. Night driving is just too much for me. In September, Dr. Feldman ordered me into the passenger seat; she gave me the names and numbers of two car services and the Visiting Nurse Association, but I never called them.

Beth Anne at the Stop 'n' Go is waddling with child. She says, "Hey," and I imagine the future life of her kid, better than I'd have predicted last spring. I have my green leafy vegetables for my eyes, romaine lettuce, broccoli, and kale, which I despise. I unload my shopping cart: a dozen jumbo carrot cake muffins for Raylene and the girls, two boxes of Animal Crackers for Lee D. and Amy, and I add some green and blue plastic cups and those disposable plates, two jugs of apple cider, and since I can't resist it, a paper tablecloth with Pilgrims, Indians, and turkeys. Jeanne had a wonderful recipe for cranberry sauce. I'll have to look it up. I'll need those wicker plate holders.

The feast is more than a week away. I have not yet so much as shared my idea with Raylene, but I am nothing if I am not all about planning. Why delay to the last minute? The murky daylight is closing down fast as a pinched candlewick as I drive home. I peer over the wheel. I bobble my head this way and that to see what I must see. If I trusted my eyes, I'd be driving between wavy lines, but that's an illusion I adjust for by driving straight. The road seems to uncurl as I crawl forward, slow and steady, my pace no problem as long as I stay off the highways.

Since Art Jones started his landscaping project, there's a backhoe on our front lawns, but I hate parking in the street; there's no telling who will come by at night. The worst part of driving anywhere is coming home. The Taurus barely fits into the driveway between our houses. I cannot manage driving the length to the rear and the garage, so I park off-center in the driveway. That creates the most space between my door and Art Jones' wall.

Tentative, fat raindrops spatter my windshield. The wind is rising. I am so intent on navigating the narrow space that I do not see the black Dodge diesel truck parked on the street up the block. But once I have parked the car and have managed to come to the rear of my car to open the trunk, I see where the truck's dome light shines on a driver in a baseball cap. He helicopters a glowing cigarette out the window to the wet street, cracks open the door of his truck, steps down carefully to grind the cigarette under his boot, and strides toward me.

James Boncoeur, returned like a bad penny.

"Can I help you with that, Mr. Evans?" he says and without waiting for my answer he reaches past me and takes the heavy jugs of cider. He can carry them with one arm. "James Boncoeur?" he says, with that smooth lilt in his voice that makes a statement a question.

"I remember you," I say as we cross my front yard.

He says he is happy that I do. "Nothing worked out in Marquette," he says. "The deck is stacked against white men everywhere. The trick is to be in your own business, not work for someone else. That's why I admire you, Mr. Evans. I do. That cleaning business . . ." He sucks his teeth. ". . . that is a working man's dream."

I unlock my door, we wipe our feet on the mat on my enclosed porch, and we make our way in past the baseball bat, through the living room and beyond the folded, hidden, playpen. We pass through the dining room where Raylene once per month dismantles my chandelier and washes each bit of glass. In my kitchen I put my packages on the slim red Formica table in the breakfast nook while James Boncoeur carefully places the cider jugs beneath the table.

"You'll recall I am looking for Raylene," he says. "And my boy? That would be Lee D."

"I do remember that," I say.

We hurry through the thickening rain and rising wind to the car for the last of my groceries. James Boncoeur stands beside me like an old friend and notes that I must be planning a large party, all those groceries for just one man. Thunder rumbles. He gently closes the trunk and he lifts the final sack. We raise our collars.

I can't just hit him with the bat. I don't know if I have sufficient strength. It might be like poking a hornet's nest.

We walk the length of the house once more, James prattling on about the Upper Peninsula and his unqualified conviction that this country is being taken over by forces that will end the American Dream. "The family, for example. Judges are dismantling the American family. A boy needs his father, wouldn't you say?"

I agree.

"So if you knew of my Raylene's whereabouts, you'd be obliged to tell me, wouldn't you?"

"Why don't you tell me what she looks like again?" I say. "Maybe she isn't using her name."

He considers me before saying, "Now, I hear over on the other side of the river, there is a cleaning girl named Raylene who works out of this address?" He places the last sack on the breakfast nook table. The Animal Crackers tumble from a bag onto the floor, but he bends to pick those up and seems to think nothing of the fact that a man in his sixties stocks up on children's cookies. "Both Mrs. Jorgensen and Mrs. Edwards, you know them?"

"I do."

He nods, happy I will not choose denial. "Both Mrs. Jorgensen and Mrs. Edwards, they say they have their homes cleaned by this Raylene each Monday. Mrs. Jorgensen in the morning. Mrs. Edwards in the afternoon. They pay Best Cleaners. Now that's you, isn't it? They say the service is terrific and that if I am looking for a girl to ask for Raylene. You are Best Cleaners. Now, that's right, isn't it?"

"It is," I say.

He nods. He is pleased by our conversation's forward progress.

"Then my Raylene might be your employee? Short woman? Reddish hair? Kind of jumpy. Green eyes. Quiet most of the time? Given to airs about herself?"

"I know her," I say. "Just started with us."

"Well all right, then. If you can supply me with her address, I can be on my way, and sorry for your trouble."

"I don't know her address," I say. "I am sorry to disappoint you."

He sits on my breakfast stool and pushes back the bill of his Expos hat with his thumb like a man who is resigned and tired of pursuing what he wants, knows he will have it, and simply is exhausted by unconscionable delays. "Mr. Evans, how can that be? I mean, a man like you? I respect you. All those business smarts. All those girls running around doing what you tell them. How is it you would not know her address?"

"James," I say. "May I call you James?"

He nods.

"Why do you root for a baseball team that no longer plays?"

He half smiles at that. "A man stays true to his first love," he says.

I nod. I lower my voice as if we might be overheard. "James, I tell you this in confidence because we are men of certain convictions. This, my friend, is a cash business. I pay the girls folding money. They come and go, so cash has certain advantages." I put my milk in my refrigerator; coffee in the pantry.

Why do these guys so love that solemn bullshit tone? As if they were part of some cloying brotherhood that shared knowledge of a higher truth, when in fact they are clueless about what makes life worthwhile: the love of a good woman, children, building something that will remain after them. I'd get these students, always men, who intoned what they said to their own chests, chins lowered to their shirts, sure that Life was not a gift or a celebration but a joyless obstacle course. They enrolled in my finance classes to learn how to beat the system, but I taught that schemes were no substitute for plans. First they'd argued, then they dropped out, sure I was part of the guvmint-jew-nigger-media conspiracy that barred men from their dreams. And their God-given right to beat women, keep their kids ignorant, and strive for a paradise that included a four-wheel drive, a muddy road, and a six-pack of Old Milwaukee.

"Why, you dog, you!" he says, grinning broadly. "You don't pay no taxes, do you?"

"Not a red cent. It used to be a great country."

He tips his hat, and runs his hand back over his head. The mullet is growing back. He has a small clip on his hair at his neck. The tattoo of the cross on his throat jumps above his collar when he throws back his head to laugh. I did not notice before, but one of his canine teeth is gold. "I admire that, sir. I do." He smoothes his hair and replaces his cap. "And Raylene?"

"I think I know where she lives," I say, "but I am damned if I know the address."

"That's not going to do," he says, and narrows his blue eyes.

"I can take you there," I say, and his face brightens.

"You will?"

"Why not?"

"That suits me, Mr. Evans. That suits me just fine. We'd best go before this storm worsens."

So he pulls up the satin collar of his Expos jacket, and I pull up the collar of my woolen jacket. We head out into the night.

It's dark. This is no longer some shadow hour. It is dark as it gets. The wind and rain are mounting. In the upper boughs, the rain slaps leaves with genuine force. We stand in the shelter of my porch as I lock my house door. As he expects to stay at Raylene's, we will need two vehicles. James will be happy to follow me in his truck. Since the truck is parked up the street beyond the oak that dominates the block, I will drive him to it. It's only a few doors down, but in this weather, "That makes the most sense," I say. We push open the screen door and sprint for my car in the narrow driveway.

As we run, I shout to him. "The driveway is too narrow for you to open the passenger side. I'll back out!" When I get to the Taurus, I shout back to him, "James, can you clear those leaves from the rear window?" I say. "And with all the construction, if you could guide me as I back out of the driveway, I'd be grateful."

He nods. "I'll clear them leaves for you, Mr. Evans. Easy enough."

I shout my thanks and climb into my car. I start the engine. I can't see a thing. I remember only shapes and light. I hold my left foot on the brake and slip the car into reverse. The car wants to jump. I near stand on the brake. As the leaves clear from my rear window, I abruptly lift my left foot from the brake and with my right press the accelerator. If James shouts a warning, I don't hear it. The wind is pretty fierce. The leaves blow. I am just a confused old man going blind, and this is wind-driven rain in November.

Confused, blind old man that I am, I run him down. Three times.

By spring, most of the mess is cleared up.

I have paid every dime required to repair and repaint the stucco side of Art Jones' house. I gouged an awful bad scar. That good, ordinary, easy-going man is a friend. I don't know why we never spoke. I like Myrtle, his wife, as well. Art's sole worry was that the construction on his yard was the cause of the accident, but I reassured him this was not the case. "It was me," I said. "Too proud to stop driving." Myrtle confided in me that tongues in the neighborhood had waggled about the short young woman who visited the old geezer so often, so I gave her the details of my oncoming blindness, now arrived, mentioned that Raylene and I had not only been business partners, but fibbed that Raylene had some training as a nurse. This satisfied Myrtle's curiosity about the comings and goings of the other women. People are saying "Hello" to me on the street, so I guess those waggling tongues have been stilled, and my status in the neighborhood has in fact climbed. Myrtle occasionally brings me whatever she has cooked. Her cooking is awful. Far too much salt, but I say, "Thanks!"

James Boncoeur required a full hip replacement. They make artificial joints from titanium. He will walk forever with a cane and a limp. He spent weeks in the hospital and will continue to need physical therapy for a long while. I am truly glad he is not dead. Since his right leg will be two inches shorter than his left, even Amy can outrun him. No one has designed an artificial retina, though I gather there is some research, which if successful will be too late for me. But good luck to them, I say.

When the time came, Dr. Feldman offered a deposition that my eyesight was shot and that I'd been cautioned to drive only in emergencies, a shade away from her actual advice, but my lawyer and I chose not contradict her. They pulled my license after my former student also by deposition told the county prosecutor about the snowy night I nearly ran her down.

My insurance company accused me of negligence for not informing them of a substantive change in my driving ability, but I had a driver's license in my wallet and no mandated state eye test to establish my inability to drive had been administered, so we remained in a gray area of law. All I need do, my lawyer maintained, is claim that I had not realized my sight had deteriorated as much as it had, which made me guilty of bad judgment, which is not negligence. Dry macular degeneration is an insistent, insidious condition, but it's hard to identify the precise day I should have decided I was blind. "And look sorry," my lawyer said. "Damned sorry."

I do not know if I managed that. I did stare at my hands.

When the D.A. learned of James' prison record for abuse, and Mrs. Jorgensen and Mrs. Edwards verified that this ex-con drifter had made inquires about his former wife in violation of his parole, the D.A. was disinclined to prosecute me for much of anything. I claimed I was trying to drive to a police station for my own safety after being threatened for not revealing Raylene's whereabouts. I was no criminal, just a befuddled, frightened, frail old man.

The mess that remains is the tort. James will sue, but my lawyer thinks he will be hard-pressed to find a jury to rule against a blind man. They will settle out of court for the limit to my liability on my car insurance. James will whine to whoever is willing to listen that the courts won't give an honest white man justice, but James is just another jerk with a mullet and a baseball cap, fan of a team that no longer exists, no less. Last I heard, he has returned to his grandmother in Quebec Province. His chances of demonstrating financial damages diminish every day he enjoys Canadian health care.

Heather and then Amber pretty much run Best Cleaners. I've lost interest, though I keep the books for them and make sure they are paid regularly. I've given them both raises as they take on more responsibility. Our Wendy had a healthy girl, eight pounds, eleven ounces. Wendy continues to work for us now and then, our first call whenever we get a special job or someone is throwing a party or something like that. Oh, and Beth Anne at the Stop 'n' Go had a boy, Frank Jr. The store manager handed out cigars. Best Cleaners continues to grow. When we hired Phyllis and Carmen, I made Heather a ten percent partner to keep her from striking out on her own, her ten percent coming from my fifty. When Heather sees our receipts she says, "It just doesn't seem possible, Mr. Bob." When our Yellow Pages ad appeared, we had a pop-and-cake party for the children.

But I have lost Raylene.

I suppose she heard a man was making inquires, and Raylene did all she knows to do: she made like a rabbit. I picture her running out into that stormy night, her children in her arms, hurling a few things into the truck, gunning the motor, popping the clutch, and wheels throwing up smoke, vanishing into the vast American night.

Winter was a long, slow plunge into darkness. The snow that fell in December was still on the ground in April. When I was not with my lawyer, once the girls had the shape-up and were gone for the day, I sat in the house by the sunniest window, but maybe because of the season, but maybe because of my eyes, each day grew darker than the day before. Night gathered too early, it seemed to me. Some days I held a book on my lap just for appearances, which is crazy. The world went cold, and I found myself thinking I would soon have to make good my promise to myself to end everything before I slid into perpetual darkness.

But three days ago I received a picture postcard from the Meramec Caverns, Jesse James's hideout in Missouri. "We are OK," is all it said, printed with red crayon in letters an inch tall. No signature. I showed it to Myrtle. God bless the woman. "Look at that," she said, "the postmark is from South Bend. That's the home of Notre Dame, Bob. They play wonderful football, don't they? We went to South Bend years ago. They have this bell tower, but South Bend is nowhere near Missouri...." and she prattled on in this vein quite a while until my kettle whistled and she refused tea, all the time me wondering how a postcard from Missouri was mailed from Indiana.

I imagined the tiny red-haired woman peering over the wheel of a diesel red pickup, hauling her children to the library to read to them, criss-crossing the country to escape a man she did not know could barely walk, saved by a man who could barely see. Was she emerging from the American night? Her half-brother was somewhere in Indiana. Might his name be Shaughnessy?

It's June. The sun shines longer each day. The trees are in bud, and I can tell that because my eyes and nose itch with new pollen. When the breeze is from the west, you can smell the farms and fields just outside of town. When I lift my face skywards, I can feel the warmth of the sun. I see flashes of light and shadow, shapes that move toward me or move away.

Against advice, I have bought a bus ticket.

I have lied to my doctor and said I am going east to New York City to visit my son; she grudgingly has admitted that journey is worth some risk. At her insistence, I carry a white cane. It folds neatly on three hinges. Dr. Feldman gave the cane to me. I've never unfolded it until today as I climbed aboard the Greyhound bus. It is early morning, not yet sunup. I damn near broke my neck on the bus steps. I tripped on the damned cane.

I am unsure I will call my son at all. The bus travels on Interstate 80, which coincidentally passes right through South Bend, the home of the Fighting Irish. I will depart this bus for a day or two to make inquiries about a cleaning girl there. Her name may be Goodheart, or Boncoeur or even Shaughnessy. My guess is to try the neighborhoods where faculty reside. Their homes are neat and liable to be filled with books.

I have a cashier's check in my pocket for $4,237.56, Raylene's share of the business profits these months passed. A debt must be paid. Just three days ago, she mailed that post-card from South Bend. She could have been passing through, but I hope not. In any event, I have to look for myself.

The driver assists me to my front seat, the first row behind him, and we set out east into the dawn. Finding Raylene will take luck, but I am a lucky man. I see that.

The Veldt

Poached and snotless eggs quiver on Samson Levy's bacon-free plate. Lillian cares about her husband's heart. She has managed his white toast to an impeccable, improbable golden brown, lightly buttered. "This is good," Samson lies. His fork stabs a yolk and yellow goo oozes to the edge of the plate where home fries should be, but are not. Forget bacon. Just forget bacon.

Fourteen days ago, fifteen counting today, Samson emptied his desk at Leaders Are Made, Inc. His accumulated personal crap came to about two cubic feet. The cardboard box is still purloined in the Lexus's trunk, safe from Lillian's eyes. Samson has yet to break the news of his dismissal to his wife. Lillian believes they both vacation at home. For once, she is half wrong.

Job search. The phrase makes his head hurt. The market for leadership trainers is less than robust; the market for people who train leadership trainers doesn't exist. He had a career; now he needs a job. Get-the-job-done Lillian deserves better. He has spared the mother of his sons the news so her time off can be carefree, but come Monday morning when they are scheduled to return to work, only one will have anywhere to go.

"Eat that, and you're ready to clear the south forty," Lillian says.

"Get my axe."

"Sam, why don't you run with me? You used to run with me. Run with me."

Slivers of egg tremble on his fork and then slide down his throat. He ought to tell her today. "I don't need exercise. My health is fine," he lies. In fact, his blood pressure has his doctor's notice. Forty-two, and Samson is borderline hypertensive, for crissakes. Blood pressure and cholesterol killed his father. What kind of medical coverage can they get from Lillian's place?

"I need you to live longer than I do," she laughs. Special K fills her bowl. Lillian's toast is dry. "I'd miss you too much."

Breakfast prepared by Lillian comes with the frequency of a solar eclipse—rare, but not impossible, spectacular when it happens. Lillian has spooned Dundee Orange Marmalade and Polaner's All Fruit Strawberry into tiny twin cylindrical clear acrylic containers. She has folded napkins to triangles. Their cotton tablecloth is arrogantly spotless. They sip orange juice from squat, genuine juice glasses. The Levys' white oak kitchen table overlooks their garden. New autumn air wafts their pale green café curtains.

This is better than the Marriott, he thinks.

The fact is that Lillian Levy rarely cooks; Lillian Levy defrosts, opens, or pours. Their pizza and Thai place are both on speed dial, and the drivers know their way to the Levy home despite a complicated route through dark suburban streets and unmarked winding lanes. Lillian Levy won't clean, can't sew, and only vaguely knows the uses of an iron. When it is her turn to do laundry, she occasionally forgets to separate whites from darks. Still, the wife he adores can describe three uses for a vacuum cleaner, none of which involve carpets or dust, two of which are not recommended for children. As if by compensation or default—Samson could not say which—Lillian has made her reputation as a Big Thinker, the Vice-President and Director of Communications for the Bates Foundation, the charitable trust improving the lives of inner city children and their mothers through entrepreneurial investment.

Not yet registered for unemployment benefits, Samson clings to what he knows is a delusion; the phone will ring to summon him back, perhaps with a raise, compensation for the terrible mistake and injustice the company perpetrated. He's mentally rehearsing his gracious and forgiving acceptance speech when movement in the tall grass at the edge of their yard catches his eye. Something out there lives, a dangerous place for anything wild. He peers at the spot. Nothing.

The thing at the edge of their garden veers his mind to last night's dream. It assaults his memory sharp as a whiff of ammonia. The dream is an old friend. He has had it many times. Sexually sated, as his body last night sank into torpor, he lay on his back and drifted in and out of his otherworld.

Bent and hurried, Lillian hunkers down in front of him. They must run. Run. Get away. Run. Run. The grass is dangerously dry. Lillian is naked. Something is out there. Something comes for them. Run. They need to make the trees. For safety's sake, they need to make the trees. Run. Run. Stay low, and run.

By an act of will, he pulls himself back to the present. "Family week was a good idea," he says. Last week, while the boys began their first full days of school, Samson and Lillian were like teenagers with over-trusting absent parents. They did it on the stairs, in the shower, and once, when Lillian snuck up on him, in the garage. They'd polished the hood of their car.

On her feet, Lillian braces her ankle on a chair frame, straightens her leg and bends her forehead to her knee. She grasps her elevated toes with two hands. Lillian's perfectly black hair is as short as his, bone dry as soon as she steps from the shower. She visits a health club three days each week in a futile attempt to harden the Mommy-pouch at her abdomen. Bearing children will do that. He tells her not to bother. This week he'll need to tell her they cannot spare the expense. Why does she want the body of a teenager? Lillian's hips were made to bear children. The rich lushness of her body makes him want to drop to his knees and weep with gratitude.

Samson Levy loves his wife; when he has dirty dreams, Lillian is in them.

Lillian yelps as she slaps open the screen door and skips down the three wooden steps to run in place on the flagstone walk, pumping her knees to her chest, elevating her heart rate for the run. Her red Nike shirt matches the crimson trim of her shoes and the pom-poms at the heels of her socks. At the property's edge, beyond the spruce and a flock of starlings, she gains speed, and her elbows pump as she sails beyond the taller grass where the live thing hides. Samson follows her with his mind's eye. Three lots away, she will stretch to longer rhythms and pick up the paved-over railroad bed that like a ruler slices through five miles of their community. Her gait will smooth. She will run and run and run.

Leaning a shoulder against the door frame, Samson watches his wife vanish into the landscape.

Lillian needs protection from truth like Mozart needed a kazoo.

Samson tosses the last of his coffee into the yard. The live thing rustles the tall grass. Everything turns out for the best, his mother liked to say.

Of course, the last time he heard her say that they were casting the first clods of damp earth clattering onto his father's coffin. But the old girl may have had a point. Samson's mother is remarried to a man who smells of Lagerfeld. They summer in the Italian Alps. Samson's father smelled of cheap cigars, and after three hours in the Abruzzi he'd have gone batshit in search of "basic American food," by which he meant a Big Mac, fries, and a vanilla shake, his ordinary lunch. At sixty-one, driving back from Buffalo, Dad's heart stopped. The Chevy continued for several hundred yards before colliding with a bridge abutment. Dad sold medical supplies, so the lesson was clear: though you hump a Chevy Impala full of stents and bandages, you cannot cheat McDeath.

The live thing stirs the line of weeds at the edge of the Levy yard. Rabbit? Squirrel? Mole? If he trapped it, could he eat it? Not that he'd want to, but perhaps it tasted like bacon.

Samson Levy is cursed to live at a time when habits developed over 250,000 years on the evolutionary mainline have become fatal. His instincts will kill him. Like his father, Samson Levy's tongue prefers the rich oils in fried foods. His teeth are designed to tear at meat. Salt tastes so good because salt is supposed to be scarce. Sweet is sweet for a reason, and fats taste smooth for a reason, and shit neither tastes nor smells like ice cream because on the evolutionary mainline we need to avoid shit whenever and wherever we encounter it.

Samson Levy has grown expert at detecting the presence of shit.

Sweet-faced, blonde Davy bounces around in the back seat of the Lexus like a marble in a rolling shoebox. Forget seatbelts. Davy may be the whitest white boy in America, but he wants hip-hop gangsta-rap, or whatever in hell they are calling it these days. His parents stay with Oldies and Classic Hits, but this fact does not inhibit their eight-year-old son who stands on the seat and postures, holding two fingers horizontally like a gun, a badass honky with a badass attitude doing his very best with Crosby, Stills, Nash and Young: Teach your mothafuckin' children well, ...

Above the granite cliff north of Route 9, the Chestnut Hill Mall gleams white in the sun, a fortress-temple from a Biblical age. Samson navigates the spiral ramps that deliver the Lexus into the concrete ziggurat that is a parking garage. In this mall, for the cost of a macadamia nut cookie, you can feed a family of four in Haiti.

Steering through Level 3A, Samson envisions the day before them. Davy will grow cranky; Lillian will buy something she believes they can afford, but which Samson knows they cannot. Then the Levys will have a small lunch at a restaurant that floats lemon slices in the water glass. He and Davy will order something with a fancy name that really is spaghetti drizzled with the cheese of a barnyard animal, possibly a goat. After critically eyeballing the menu and questioning a waiter on the exact preparation of two or three tempting items—all of which will be cooked with too much oil—Lillian will order Cobb, Greek, or Garden salad. Dressing on the side. Who can screw up lettuce?

The Levys wait while a woman at the wheel of a white Mercedes SL with glowing brake lights starts her engine, adjusts her rear view mirror, and brushes back her hair with the palm of her hand. She readjusts the rearview mirror only after she is satisfied with her looks. She reaches down and to her right, fumbling with what must be her purse, and comes up with a pack of cigarettes. She moves with the deliberation of a glacier. The Levys wait more. Her window drops as she exhales a cloud of blue smoke.

"Do not honk the horn," Lillian says. "Do not." In the backseat, Davy does his trampoline workout. The kid may mature to be a dolphin. Maybe he can be Davy's agent, get him a job at Sea World.

The Mercedes crawls an inch, then jerks a few painful inches more. It takes the Mercedes three tries to create maneuvering space sufficient to exit. As the car passes them, Samson can't help but see the crone's dyed copper hair, her smear of lipstick, her eyebrows no more than so much paint. She's a death mask bent low over the wheel, and the sight of her is so startling that Samson hesitates.

Naturally, in that heartbeat of hesitation, a blue Mazda RX-7, top down, snaps smartly into the parking space.

The driver can't be twenty-two. Twisted in the Mazda's seat, the little putz flashes a grin at Samson and kills his engine.

"Don't," Lillian says, but her far-off voice hardly registers over the blood thundering in his ears. It's like running crouched through the weeds. It's all instinct now.

Samson leans most of his body out his window to shout, "You're kidding, right?" Maybe Lillian reaches for him; there's no saying. Nothing is under control. Runrunrunrun. Samson kills the ignition, pinches open his safety belt, punches open his door, and in a single fluid movement stands beside his car.

The kid is already walking away. Muscled, young, his crimson golf shirt trimmed with gold is cut so that it flaps loosely at his exposed, hard waist. There's spring in the little bastard's step. Samson wears baggy cutoffs. Threads flutter about his bare knees. His faded t-shirt was a gift from the exec board of a promising dot-com that invested in leadership training in preparation for their imminent expansion just before they crashed and burned in a spectacular bankruptcy. Their final asset was a foosball table.

"Sam!" Lillian calls. She says other things. Samson cannot hear her.

"Back in five minutes," the kid calls over his shoulder. He can hear that. Oh, Samson hears that just fine. "I just need tennis balls."

"You think I should wait?" Heat fills Samson's face. Anger is a tourniquet at his throat.

The kid breaks into a sprint.

The *Leaders Are Made* manual calls this an LCP, a Leadership Choice Point. Receding before him is a totally arrogant asshole who needs killing, but Samson wrote the *LAM* manual and so he knows that any hormonal response to stress lasts no more than three seconds. It's all on page 38. Heart rate soars; blood pressure follows, but after those initial three seconds, the mind can reassert itself. Fight or flight responses are instinctive, wholly human, but effective leaders seek the third option, the LCP.

Rage drains from Samson like dirty dishwater.

Back in the car, Lillian pats his wrist as he turns the ignition key, and as if by reward, Fate compensates his self-control. An aisle away, an engine starts. Davy laughs as centrifugal force hurls the boy across the car seat when Samson circles into the correct parking aisle. This time, there is no competition.

The mall itself is a temple of cool marble, gold fixtures, and sparkling chrome. Lillian is talking copper-bottomed pots and pans for meals she will never cook. Davy wants to know if the pizza is good here. Davy eats anything, anywhere, anytime. The kid might be hollow. But this day Samson hardly notices the polished surfaces, the silent escalators, and the artificial public spaces. Instead, this day, though he is out of the hormonal storm of anger, he chooses to focus on the jerk in the blue Mazda. It's a choice. Why let the moment go? Where's the satisfaction in it? What about justice?

He releases Davy's hand. "It's not enough," he mutters, and to Lillian says, "I left something in the car. I'll catch up to you."

His wife calls after him, "Don't do this," but Samson is already at a near-sprint to the garage elevator.

The garage air is foul with auto exhaust. The black plastic dome of a ceiling security camera is maybe thirty yards off, but the blue Mazda just might be in a blind spot. He'll need to take special care.

Samson is genuinely relaxed. He operates on instinct, yes, but it is deliberated action. His blood is cold. This is leadership. Leadership in a new direction, but nevertheless leadership.

At the Mazda, Samson kneels as if to tie a shoe. From this spot, at this height, he sees no ceiling camera. Unless their cameras can see around corners, his luck is with him.

Twelve years and screwed. A tiny wrinkle in the economy, and the sons of bitches who were happy to let him create their business suddenly cannot afford him. Sure, all across America mid-level execs were being incinerated like underbrush to slow an engulfing firestorm, but where did they come off firing him?

He unfastens the valve cap of the Mazda's right front tire; his fingers come away grimy. He spits on his thumb. What was it Lillian had called after him? Don't do this? He needs to do this more than he needs to breathe and eat.

Air hisses slowly around his fingers, but the tire stays round. He tries squeezing it, but the rubber is hardly as soft as a bicycle's tube. He moves to restore circulation in his lower legs and his keys jingle. He still uses the key chain his older son, Michael, gave him for Father's Day, what? ten years ago?

The Leaders Are Made office key is the largest in the ring. That crew of quick-hit buccaneers did not have the smarts to ask for the return of his key. He ought to pull up some night and greet Freddy, the security guard, before helping himself to five or six computers. Hell, Freddy would help Mr. Levy carry the stuff out.

He presses the point of his office key into the valve. The aroma of vulcanized rubber and stale air teases his nose. The key is better than his fingernail, but the tire simply isn't deflating fast enough. All right, so no phone call and apology were coming soon. But what were they thinking? Did they expect to find some twenty-two-year-old tennis-playing snot in a crimson shirt that could do his job for half his pay by reading his manual?

His back aches. He straightens up; at the elevator, two women in heels and shorts walk past, but they hardly notice him at all.

Samson won't put sugar or a burning rag into the gas tank. Samson will smash no headlamps. The windshield will stay intact. Pissing onto the convertible's seat has appeal, but is just a touch beyond what this considered LCP calls for. Not a violent man by nature, Samson is well aware he skirts the brink of an abyss. Better to leap than fall. A choice. There are no accidents.

He should have said something. Anything. Instead, he meekly loaded his stuff and skulked out of the place like a beaten dog. To save their own worthless hides, they'd pushed Samson to the herd's edge and left him for the jackals.

He wants to cripple the Mazda. He thinks how his bright yellow road emergency kit is in his car's trunk beside the box of his stuff, the framed pictures of Lillian and the boys. Tools. Tools separate us from the animals. We're slower, weaker and less adaptable, but boy oh boy oh boy, how we like tools and that good old opposable thumb for that evolutionary advantage.

Samson saunters to his Lexus. He chirps the alarm and pops the trunk. No one can just open a car anymore; it has to wink and engage in an electronic dialogue. Car alarms —who or what was being alarmed? Who heard a car alarm and called the police? All they did was notify the neighborhood that some asshole did not know how to unlock his car, or that the alarm itself was broken. They never, never, indicated theft. What kind of survival mechanism was that? But a good Phillips-head screwdriver; well, that was another story.

The screwdriver's vulcanized grip feels right in his fist. Jesus, how he loves the feel of tools. Back beside the Mazda, the screwdriver handle becomes moist in his hand. He looks over his shoulder, and with his knees bent just so, he swings his arm past his own hip. It's a backhand shot. The tennis player would appreciate that.

The screwdriver's point strikes the tire sidewall and bounces harmlessly off the sidewall.

That's all right. Anything this fulfilling ought to require muscle and follow-through that calls for sinew and bone.

The second time, his hip braced against the fender, when he swings his arm down and backward the effort actually lifts him off his feet. The screwdriver's point barely penetrates the tire sidewall, but this blow is a certain kill. He works the tool a bit, widening the wound. When the sidewall rips, there is no explosion, but the final expiration from the tire sussurates the sigh of Death itself. The screwdriver dangles in the gash as air streams weakly around it. The tire collapses, and the Mazda finally, satisfyingly, lists, brought down and crippled.

Naturally, at that moment, the crimson-shirted tennis player appears at the elevator. The guy swings a plastic bag— tennis balls, for sure.

"The foursome may be delayed," Samson thinks as he squats lower to scuttle away. When he straightens up, the tennis player is ten yards before him, closing fast, grinning like a birthday balloon. Samson can make out the stitching on his chest. Harvard. He'd be playing tennis at Longwood, the nearby country club. Harvard. Of course.

To look away would be fatal. The jerk is still grinning, but his face swirls puzzlement. From where does he know this guy coming toward him? At five feet, Samson nods imperceptibly. As they pass shoulder to shoulder, Harvard does the same, as if they were old friends. Giddily, Samson considers striking up a conversation. They could exchange business cards, except for the facts that Samson's phone has been disconnected and his only occupation is to survive.

Once Samson passes the guy, he quickens his pace. He's still heel-toe, but he readies for a dead run. It won't be five, maybe ten seconds before Harvard sees what there is to see.

Samson makes the elevator plaza, swings open the glass door, barely feels the rush of air-conditioning on his face. He swings into the stairwell as he hears a wail of loss. The fire door booms shut behind him. He yields to his panic. Run, run get away Runrunrunrun.

Hauling ass up the stairs two at a time, he pauses at the first stairwell landing. He hears nothing, but as he takes the next landing he hears the metal fire door below boom open.

The chase is on.

In his dream, he keeps low and move move move. So this is old stuff. He's been here a million times; his DNA has been here a million more. He feels his pulse in his scalp. Blood pressure? Hypertension? Oh, doctor! He is as alive as he can be! After two weeks of gloom, the chase is exhilarating. He wonders: other than shoplifting, is there a way to get paid for this?

Samson pivots on the ball of his foot, takes the next landing, swings around and realizes he'll have to outthink his younger pursuer. This is part of the game. What's the point of experience and age if you don't get cagey?

Instead of headlong flight, he lunges out a door and pops into the first floor of the garage. Palms against the cold metal, he carefully, softly, closes the steel door behind him. A two second investment in stealth will yield much more time to escape. He moves among cars, fast enough to cover ground but not so fast as to draw attention to himself on a security monitor. Sunlight beckons to him from outside. A tree lies in stark silhouette against the blue sky.

The little jerk will charge up the stairs into the mall itself, counting on his youth and speed to overtake his prey, when all the while Samson will have sidestepped the chase.

Samson's heart slows. For propriety's sake, he retucks his shirt into his waistband, cooling down as he walks the circular gravel path to the mall's pedestrian entrance. It's a lovely day. It would not have done to have taken the elevator. Oh, no, the doors might open and there might be Harvard waiting for him. Samson has better instincts than to be boxed in.

Lillian sits on the marble lip of a bubbling fountain near the food court. The blue tile bottom of the round pool sparkles with quarters and dimes. For the patrons of the Chestnut Hill Mall, the chlorinated pool reproduces the magic of Rome's Trevi fountain. Yeah, right. Like Rome, but in a mall.

Samson joins Lillian.

"You did something stupid."

"Depends on how you look at it. Davy?"

His wife points to the kid in line for ice cream. Davy waves, his little fist clutching a few bills. Samson scoops enough water from the fountain into his hand to wet his face. He wipes his hands on his shirt. Lillian gives him a tissue. He presses his forehead dry.

When he opens his eyes, Harvard's finger is inches from his face.

"That's the man!"

The mall security guard restrains Harvard with an out-stretched arm. Samson doesn't let himself smile. It's another LCP, all right. Samson opts for puzzlement and denial. He says to Lillian, "The quarters and dimes in this thing must come to a hundred dollars."

"That's the man!" Harvard repeats, practically squealing.

Runrunrunrun, but Lillian's hand at his back, just a touch, helps him keep still.

"You slashed my tire, you fuck!"

Lillian blanches like the Mother Superior of the Sisterhood of Impeccable Purity. Last night, she'd have shamed a street whore in Amsterdam, but this Saturday afternoon she is scandalized by profanity. "Don't curse in front of my wife, fella," Samson says easily.

The unarmed guard's khaki uniform makes him a cred-
ible rent-a-cop. He has handcuffs and is burly enough to handle anyone he ordinarily might have to—teenage shoplifters
or errant Harvard tennis players. "Sir, did you damage this
man's car?"

"Not me. Not possible. I've been here all day."

Davy ambles over. The ball of vanilla ice cream already
melts over the edge of his waffle cone. It drips gooily onto his
hands. He's got multi-colored jimmies, as many stuck to his
lips as to the ice cream. That's Davy for you. More mess than
nourishment, and go for the good parts first. How will he
provide for his sons? Samson grasps his boy and protectively
cages him behind his arms and legs.

"I saw you!" Harvard shrieks.

His tone defeats him, Samson knows. Harvard should
enroll for some leadership training. He sounds like an hys-
terical girl, while Samson, Lillian and David Levy are a reas-
suring Norman Rockwell reverie.

Lillian says to the guard, "Sam and I have been in the
mall all day with our son." She tousles Davy's hair. The boy
grins. His tongue lolls about his ice cream.

"They're lying!"

It's too wonderful seeing the little jerk turn purple with
indignation. A small crowd gathers. Samson stays non-con-
frontationally seated. Lillian's hip presses his. He holds Davy
closer.

The potbellied guard has a Lebanese nose, and the weari-
ness in his eyes is the sure indication that he works this security job only on weekends for a few extra bucks. He does not
need this shit from a kid who goes to Harvard. "Maybe you
saw someone else," the guard suggests. It is no question.

Lillian stands. "Officer," she says, "I appreciate your ef-
forts, but I am not going to subject our son to any more of
this. We've been together since we arrived. The three of us."

"Right," Davy says and licks the cone. "Me, Mommy and Daddy."

The guard turns to Harvard. "There's nothing on surveillance tape. You saw camera 11. We looked with you. Did you physically witness this guy cut your tire?"

"I told you, no. But he was walking away..."

"What floor of the garage?" Samson asks.

"Three," the guard says.

"Did we park on three?" Samson asks Lillian.

"I think so."

It's an interesting moment. What can the guy say? I recognize you and your lovely family from when I screwed you out of a parking space.

Lillian sighs. "This is ridiculous," she says. She takes Samson's hand and pulls him to his feet. She reaches easily into her bag and gives the guard her business card. "If you need to contact us, here's my information. However, if you give my name to this man, I will sue you and the mall. The card is exclusively for your convenience. Do we understand each other?"

"Lady, I don't want your card," the guard says, pulling back his hand. Liability suits danced to his left and right. Ah, Lillian, the Big Thinker.

They've made it. They are in the tall trees beyond the grass. Lillian replaces her card in her purse.

"Then you'll understand that I'd appreciate your staying with this man until we are safely away. I don't want a lunatic stalking my child," Lillian says. She bends to lift Davy. She hated carrying the kids when they were little. I am not some goddam gorilla, she'd say. Pearly white vanilla glazes Davy's face. It's sticky in his hair, and it sticks to Lillian's cheek. She probably has not lifted Davy for at least three years.

The small crowd seems pleased at this victory for family values. Nobody likes anyone from Harvard, anyway.

"Holy shit!"

"Hey, fella, that's enough of that," the guard says. The crowd nods agreeably.

At the elevator, as Lillian drops Davy to the floor, Samson whispers, "Nice show."

"Don't push it, bucko" she says. Her nostrils are distended, her bloodless lips thin.

Very late that night, close to morning in truth, Lillian awakens when she thinks she hears a sound. Samson is not beside her. His place is cold. She waits a bit, hoping to hear him stir in the bathroom, but there is nothing. Rolling to her hip, Lillian hugs a pillow and waits, but after thirty minutes it is plain Samson is not returning from wherever he is. She slips her feet into mules, wraps herself in her thin cotton robe and makes her way from the bedroom. This, she thinks, is it.

Passing the boys' rooms at the head of the stairs, she peeks in. She likes this life. She heard Michael come in after one and take milk. Her teenager might have been with a girl. Well, why not? Michael's room is ankle deep in clothing. With his air-conditioner turned to the highest setting, he is a huddled mass below several blankets. David, her baby, as always sleeps with his arms and legs spread wide, flat on his back, his carefree face visible to her. Like a Rembrandt, his face is luminous with a light all its own. She needs no light to see David's face anywhere, anytime. Yes, she loves Michael, but in her heart her baby is her favorite. So close to sleep, she can admit this to herself. God, yes, how she likes this life.

The cold in the kitchen floor penetrates the soles of her slippers. She expected to find Samson here, murmuring on the telephone, so she is only a little surprised to see the rear door to the yard open. It's a warm enough night. She goes down the wooden steps to the yard.

He husband squats on the grass at the far edge of the property. He holds a flashlight. He has some other stuff. It is too dark for her to make out what. His back is toward her.

She says. "What's up?"

"Something is living in our garden."

"Rabbit?"

"Probably." He does not turn to face her.

The neighbors' houses on both sides loom dark. The air is chilled with oncoming autumn. She does not look forward to going back to work. She asks, "Sam, what's going on?"

"I need more tools if I am going to get it."

"Get what?"

"Whatever it is."

She gathers the cloth of her robe beneath her and kneels beside him. He's in boxer trunks and a T-shirt. "Do you have to get it?"

"It's on our land." He pauses, as if to realize more needs to be said. "I thought I might freeze it with the light and just grab it with my hands, but I think I will need a snare. I don't need to kill it. I want to take it someplace safe."

The night smells different from the day, she thinks. "Sam, is there anything you need to tell me?"

"Something is alive out here."

Her hand reaches for his shoulder. "You're worrying me," she says.

"I've been fired," he says after a short pause. "I was going to tell you in the morning." He turns to face her and sits directly on the damp ground. "I am so sorry, Lil. I did nothing wrong. They just fired me. There's not enough money coming through the company's door."

"When?"

"Two weeks ago."

It is hard to see him in the darkness. "You should have told me," she says and immediately sees why he did not. She might well have done the same. Tomorrow they will work on his resumé. It's Sunday—that means the big Help Wanted section. Good. There's the executive recruiting service that has been sniffing around her: she'll offer Sam up on Monday. "You should have told me," she repeats.

Her arm circles his shoulders. His head rests against her breast. "I am so sorry, Lil."

Lillian holds him. Men know so little of what women will guess or imagine. Samson has been distant and strange; Lillian thought it was his health or another woman. All she knows about men she learned from her father, and what she learned about men is that what men will do is leave. But after that business today at the mall, she imagined far, far worse. For two weeks, she's done everything she knows to do to keep him—sex, food, food and sex—and it turns out he simply needs her. Once again, she sees how Samson is a far, far better man than her father. She should have thought. "Life could be worse," she says. "We'll work on it."

"The bastards."

"The bastards," she repeats.

At that precise moment, far to Lillian's left, the thing that lives in the yard watches them with its round black eyes and does not so much think as know how this and every other place is very dangerous, and it knows, but does not quite think, how it will be hard to return to the burrow while the Levys are in the garden but any other burrow is much too far away and in this garden there is much nourishment maybe more than any other garden on the hill so all that can be done is to wait and wait and not move and watch through very black seldom-blinking eyes while the Levys sit on the grass and hold each other and make sounds until they return to be safe in their house where they nurture their young.

All in the big garden in the night know these truths: Keep silent. Keep together. Seek shelter. Run close to the earth.

Lighted Windows

With a wave of his hand more affectionate than dismissive, he dismisses her argument. "My grandfather claimed you stood on 42nd Street at Times Square, eventually you'd see everybody you ever met."

"What's that supposed to mean? I don't get it." She toys with the three-inch quartz at her throat. She has topaz in her purse. Malachite in her pocket. Her defenses, such as they are, are with her.

"Try it this way," he says. "You sit and surf stations, color on the screen catches your eye, maybe a face, you stop. You hold it 'til you're bored, never more than a minute, then thumb the remote again. Hours pass. Afterward, can you describe what you saw? Did you truly see anything?" He shrugs, purses his lips, lifts his hands palm up—his most New York gesture—and slumps lower on the bench.

Pigeons study them, flutter up, go about their business. Tough pigeons. Arrogant pigeons. Pigeons that might be connected. Homeboy gangbanging pigeons. You have to be careful. This is a dangerous place. Any place can be. Danger is everywhere.

"I still don't get it." She laughs apologetically, trying to please. She is young. So is he, but not so much.

He sighs. "All right. Try this. When I was a kid, everyday I took the train to my high school. An elevated. They don't rely on those yellow buses in New York City. Kids get passes to public transportation. Winters, coming home when it was dark early, I'd look out across the tracks to where people lived. But I could see only into lighted windows. Most were dark. You see what I mean?"

"You can only see where there is light. I get that. But what kind of people?"

Only a little annoyed, he says, "Women in pink slips standing at a stove. Little kids in grimy T-shirts. Guys in undershirts smoking cigarettes. Old people leaning on the casements, watching the train pass. These were the lighted windows at the backs of brick tenements. Clotheslines. Tiny square gardens. Wooden fences. Like that. I was a kid, I tried to make sense of the windows. Three together would make up a story. The windows shouldn't come together like that, they have nothing to do with each other, but when I saw them quick right next to each other, they did. I saw stuff, guys yelling, women crying, but the train never stopped and pretty quick they were gone. The train never waits. That didn't stop me, though. I saw what I saw."

She shakes her head. He sighs. He really wants her to understand, so he tells her, "Okay. So try this.

"One New Year's morning, near four in the morning, after a party, I stop for coffee. Cafeteria in Brooklyn. I'm done, walk out through the revolving door, this Hispanic woman in a red dress runs by so fast she almost knocks me down. Her dress sparkles. All sequins. Low cut. She has an enormous chest and she bounces when she runs. She's no kid. Maybe forty-five, maybe even fifty. The dress is slit up the back, but only so far. She has to run from the knees down. And she's barefoot, except for stockings, the seams thick as your little finger. Thing is, she can't lift her hem to run faster because both her hands are clapped over her face and there's a web of blood flowing through her fingers down her wrists to her elbows. All I see over her hands is her black eyes, wide. This is a flash. Like a strobe photo. She gets past me and makes it to the center of Church Avenue. Cars on both sides of her. New Year's morning and she's in the middle of four lanes, shivering on the double yellow centerline. She is screaming.

"A guy in a robin's-egg-blue tuxedo, black velvet lapels, comes tearing around the same corner. Bandito mustache. Hair slick. He runs in patent leather shoes with the big silver buckles, no easy trick on a frozen sidewalk. Pink shirt, all ruffles down the front. He holds the knife way out in front of him. Biggest damn thing I ever saw. The handle is red, probably plastic. All down his tuxedo sleeve, all over his pink shirt cuff, are streamers of blood.

"He catches her right there on the double yellow line. She screams 'Dios, por favor, Esteban, por favor,' then just shrieks, no words, one bare foot stamping the ground as she holds her hands out to him, her face all running blood.

"Four more guys wearing matching tuxedos tear around the corner. They slide in their slick shoes on frozen slush. I duck into a doorway and find I am standing on a crackling frozen puddle of piss. I'd call 911, but I have no phone. Do I look like I carry a phone?"

She admits he does not.

"Like pallbearers in a hurry, these four guys haul a metal garbage can. The guy with the knife turns to face them. The knife wavers back and forth, slow as a cobra. Steam comes off all of them, five men and one bleeding woman, steam like mist off horses in the morning. The woman screams and screams. Terrible to hear. One guy lifts the garbage can over his head. His opened tuxedo jacket is lined with black satin, and I think bat wings. It's funny the details you remember. The can hits the knife-guy on the shoulder, rolls off, hits the ground and booms like a church bell. He staggers, shakes off the hit, then lunges at the belly of guy who threw the can.

"You know on television how a man gets stabbed? He claps his hand over the spot wound he's trying to hold in his guts? Looks down at the spot, looks at the person who stabbed him with this astonished look on his face, maybe smiles ironically like he finally is in on some cosmic joke, then looks down one more time before he crumples really slowly to his knees and then finally falls forward?"

"I've see that," she says, happy to finally make a connection. "I've seen that."

"Well, that's bull. This guy slaps the street like a sack of wet shit dropped from the fifth floor. Blink, you missed it."

"What happened?"

"Someone pulled a fire alarm. Trucks showed up. An ambulance. I left. Went home."

"I mean, what had the woman done?"

"Beats me."

"She must have done something." When he says nothing she asks, "Well, how badly was she hurt?"

"I told you all I saw."

They were walking now. When she asks, he will not tell her his astrological birth sign.

Still, he wants her to understand in his way, so instead, he says, "All right. Listen. Try one more.

"One time, I am in Greenwich Village. This is so long ago that everything has changed. I'm on my way to class at NYU. Me. Imagine that. South of Washington Square in those days the streets each have two or three chess parlors. Pay for play. Like bowling in Buffalo. But chess. I stare in the windows. Smoke so thick you can't see the opposite wall. Old men with cloth caps, cigarettes between their thumbs and index fingers, palms up. Beside the boards these guys have chess clocks, a wooden box with two time mechanisms in it. One player moves, depresses a switch, makes the other player's clock run. Only one player's clock can run at a time. A player has to beat his opponent in just so much time.

"I go in. To see what's what, you understand?"

She nods, though she has no idea what he means.

"I take black coffee, thick as maple syrup, and drop in a clove, just like I see another guy do. Coffee is free, but I put a quarter in the dish, anyway. I know less than doo-dah about chess. I look at inlaid wood boards. I look at chess pieces. Pewter, copper, stone, quartz, ivory. A guy with three very long hairs rooted above his left ear combed all the way across his bald head offers to arrange a game for me. His accent's thicker than his coffee. I don't want to embarrass myself, I tell him. He shrugs. Says, 'Watch. Learn.'

"It's a pleasant place to be, this storefront set with three rows of narrow tables, chessboards, straw bread baskets full with green felt-bottomed plastic pieces ready for a game, a place smelling of Christmas spices, anise, and tobacco. Immobile as stone, players hunch over their boards, weight on their forearms, sweaters worn through at the elbows, only their eyes moving, quick, this way, that. They suck in the game through their eyes. It's intense. When a player makes a move, the spectators whisper, pull at their lower lips and ear lobes and hold their noses. When it comes to the other guy's folly, everybody's an expert. It's freezing outside. Dark. The chess parlor's windows run condensation, and at the seams near the walls, the droplets freeze. The ice sparkles. All you can see of the street is the glow of white, green, and red lights, pulse like colored jellyfish on fogged glass.

"I'm there half an hour when a big man, very fat, comes in. He has a boy with him, a Negro boy, maybe eighteen years old. The boy is emaciated. Bones at his wrist strain against his skin. Hair cut very close to his head. Sleepy eyes, but the cords in his neck bulge like he's angry and screaming, which he isn't, but should be. The boy looks like he escaped from Ethiopia or Zimbabwe or Somalia or some other place where food is only a good idea, not something anybody eats. He wears cheap, unlaced, high-top black sneakers, and his pants legs are so short, I see he wears no socks. When the door opens, cold air washes across the floor like cold water on an incoming tide, but this skinny kid wears no socks.

"The big man sits at a table and the black boy stands behind him. The bald guy scowls and says something to a companion. He says it loud, but he says it in maybe Bulgarian, maybe Romanian, maybe Hungarian, maybe Russian. One of those languages.

"A young guy, a student—he has a khaki back pack and a light blond beard and wears silver wire-rimmed bifocals—asks if the fat man wishes to play. I never noticed him. This young guy sits alone in the corner, under a yellow electric lamp studying a chess book. The fat man waves at him to sit and all the old guys in the place sigh as if God answers their prayers. They exchange a look, grateful for the good fortune that brings them to this place at this time. I've seen this look before. Pool rooms. Certain basketball courts uptown. Maybe front-row fans at boxing matches exchange this look. I wouldn't know about that. Tickets cost.

"They set the double chess clocks for five minutes each, which means no game can take longer than ten. The chess pieces move so quickly, the game changes so fast you'd think the pieces were alive. Knights rescue queens. Pawns die to save the king. The players slap down pieces and whack the chess clock button.

"You probably think watching chess is like watching grass grow, but it is very exciting. An old guy tells me that to play chess with so little time is called blitzkrieg, lightning war, and I can see why. The clocks tick, and the room is so quiet you think the ticking is a heartbeat. These guys, when they make a move, no one holds his nose. Not once. They nod with new understanding. They rub their chins.

"The student strokes his light beard with his knuckles while he thinks. He cups his chin in the palms of his hands. The big man tugs at a tuft of gray hair that grows thick as weed from his ear. But over the board their hands hover like hummingbirds and strike like hawks. Suddenly the fat man says, 'Clock!'

"The student's time is expired. He sighs, gives the man a dollar, and the guy hands it to the black boy. The black boy folds the bill and slides it into his jeans jacket pocket. He folds the bill as if it is an important assignment. Sharp corners, exactly matched edges. He has no socks, and his skin stretched across his face looks thinner than a balloon stretched over a plaster skull, but he is fastidious about money.

"They set the pieces up again, colors reversed, but before they start the second round, the older chess player produces a pint bottle of wine in a brown paper bag. He takes it from the inside of his quilted vest. He tilts back his head, unscrews the cap, and takes a swallow could drain the reservoir if this guy ever tasted water. His Adam's apple bobs under white stubble. The wine's fruity aroma overpowers the smoke and coffee and spices. He smacks his lips, all purple, belches softly, then drinks a second time.

"When the fat man takes the second swig, the bald man with long hair says something in Bulgarian—or Romanian. Whatever. Several old men laugh, but more shake their heads with sadness.

"Then the student and the wino begin again, just as before, but more intense. This time, the big guy wins when the student in the John Lennon glasses stops the clocks and surrenders. He hands a dollar over the board, and the fat guy passes it backward over his head to the black boy. Just as before, the black boy carefully folds it and slips it into his breast pocket.

"They play again and again. The wino drinks more and more. Still, the student can't win. He reaches into his backpack for more money. They double the stakes, but money isn't at issue. Anyone can see this is not about money. Sometimes the student loses on time. Sometimes he resigns, stopping the clocks and tipping his king. He never allows himself to be checkmated. After each loss, he extends his hand to the fat man, who never takes it.

"Comes a game, several of the old guys lean forward. Eyebrows rise. Mouths are O's. They push in to see more clearly. Seems the fat man's game is lost. He has few pieces left, no more than seconds on his clock, and each move the student makes has a ferocious finality. But then the wino lifts his queen with a kind of backhand grip, and with the same hand in one move scoops up his opponent's pawn, slaps the piece onto the square, and belches, 'Check.' It's the only word he utters other than 'clock.' No one breathes. All you can hear is the ticking. The student removes his spectacles, pinches the bridge of his nose, rubs his eyes, all while his time runs. He captures the queen, and the wino's hand, quicker than you can say it, snatches a rook, slaps it onto the board, and whacks the clock. It's another free piece. The student takes nearly forty-five seconds to respond. He chews his lip, his hand trembles over a knight, withdraws, hangs over a bishop, returns to the original knight. He's got choices. He captures the wino's rook, but when the wino pushes a pawn forward, all the old guys drop back and sigh. The student sits erect, rubs his chin, then nods his head and sags a bit. He seems smaller. His king lies on its side.

"Even the bald Bulgarian applauds. The fat man unscrews his bottle's gold cap, and he lifts the bottle to his lips. The back of his neck is puckered with boils, the collar of his shirt is rimmed with grime, and the line of gray hair behind his ears is slick with grease.

"The student is stunned by the sudden loss from what must have felt like victory. His skin is wax, lips bloodless, a tremor shakes his jaw. He's like a spoiled kid beaten at Ping-Pong by a merciless adult. You know, the kid thinks he is terrific, he's never lost, and all of a sudden he sees the adult world has been holding him safe from harm, his sense of mastery is a lie, his competence an illusion. He's not extraordinary. He's just a kid.

"He hoists his book bag on his shoulder and leaves the chess parlor. No one stops him, not even for payment. Outside, the world is hushed and indifferent. Light snow falls.

"Inside, the fat guy finishes his bottle. His eyes are puffed shut, his face is red, his nose runs. He reaches over his shoulder as if to grab the black boy's shirt, but he cannot find it. Same hands never missed a chess piece no more than three inches high, he can't find a kid six feet tall standing behind him. The black boy bends to put his ear near the fat man's lips, nods and goes sockless into the quiet snow night.

"The Bulgarian says something, but nobody laughs. The customers twirl scarves around their necks, tug tweed caps over their eyes, shrug into old coats, clap one another's shoulders, rub their hands together, and head for the door. The drunk wobbles on his seat like a bottom-heavy doll. He waits, stupefied. His green work pants are dark where he has soiled himself.

"And that moment, I realize why he never took the younger player's hand. Blind drunk, he sees nothing, least of all the student's hand in front of his face. I realize the guy never sees the chessboard. The game takes place in his mind. Move and countermove, gambit and attack, it plays like a movie in his head. A perfect movie. All he has to know over the board is the student's last move. After that, he sees farther and with more clarity than anyone. He just sees farther than anyone else. This, then that, then that, and then this must happen. On his chessboard, effects have causes. There's an inevitable chain. It must be beautiful to see. He's an artist."

"Did the black kid come back? What were they to each other?"

"I was late for my class, already missed my dinner. I left."

"That's it?"

"All I know."

"Then I still don't get it," she says mournfully. "I'll never get it." She touches the firestone set in her ring. It is no safeguard against her encroaching terror.

Later, alone, home, she remains unsettled, restlessly moving from room to room until at her table she fans her deck. His coloring, he'd have to be the King of Pentacles. She shuffles the Tarot, lays the cards out in a Celtic Cross with a Tree of Life beside it.

But the cards refuse to come together to make a tale. Nothing matches what she knew of him. The cards remain no more than isolated, pretty cards.

In desperation, she takes from her deepest desk drawer the yellow pad and a soft pencil. She thinks a bit, then invents the laughing woman, her crystals, her companion, the pigeons. She invents a bench, a man to put on it, subways, blank brick tenement walls, and lighted windows. All of it. She invents all of it. Ash cans and knives and chess players. Storefront glass and tweed caps. The Tarot deck. Even the King of Pentacles. She invents every detail.

And when she is done inventing, she writes this story so we might read it.

That helps, but only a little.

Fishhook

Every few days this guy comes into the store, and by peeping through a rack of tennis shirts or over a shelf of running shoes I spy on him. He is cautious, never buys anything, just idles in golf, or tennis, or fishing tackle. Like any other store, our inventory figures never match sales, and though I've seen him take stuff, I am not going to say a word. Shoplifting is just a sport. You're on one side or the other—those who sell and those who steal— and you do what you are supposed to do.

Last April my father decides that what I need even more than summer school is a job. This makes no economic sense. I attend the only private college that will have me, and they charge tuition at a rate that could dent the national debt. My father pays every dime, and believe me, he can afford it. I have no loans, and that's a comfort, but as my advisor says, motivation is a problem for me. They say when you have no destination, all road are the same.

With just a single semester of summer school I will graduate on time. Without it, my father will have to pay for an extra year of tuition because of a single F. The plagiarism wasn't my fault; the stupid research service forgot the footnote. But my monomaniac father calls up his old buddy and zap, here I am, snared in Roger's Sporting Life. So no summer school, and if I am in luck I will earn one-fifth of what the extra semester will cost him. You go, Dad.

Selling sucks until I notice Lightfingers Louie. He wears this bulky rat-white golf jacket I know is for boosting. He stands besides a table covered by sweatsocks, his eyes behind his wire-frame rimless glasses shift left and right, and when he leaves, Louie is several sweatsocks ahead of the game, his jacket just a bit more bulky.

Roger warns me to keep an eye on that guy. Louie snatches racquetballs. One second the cans are on the shelf, the next they aren't. The guy has hands like a vacuum cleaner. He's built like no racquetball player I've ever seen. His gut is a swallowed basketball and his pants up over his waist. I figure he's either a klepto, really likes to be in dangerous places, or he is into flea market free enterprise. I keep an eye on him, all right. I keep an eye on him all the way out of the store.

Two days later when Roger is at lunch and our cashier is out sick, which means that she is at the lake with a boyfriend, Louie reappears in the same khaki pants and same rat-white golf jacket with the big pockets. He circles a pallet of T-shirts. Roger bought forty pounds of the things, all sizes and colors with trendy expressions on them that are no longer trendy. If he sells half of them at $5.95 each, he will double his money.

Business is just a scam. The time I told my father I am a socialist, he laughed and asked if I wanted to return his charge cards.

What is it with fathers? There is no pleasing them.

Lightfingers Louie times his visit for Roger's lunch, and I can see how this is a good game plan. Fewer defenders to contend with. I am at the front register. Casually, I let my finger tease the security buzzer like a nipple attached upside down beneath the counter. A touch, and the security guards will be down on this guy like the wrath of God. I look out to the mall's milling crowds, and then I turn fast and look right at Louie.

He freezes like a deer in headlights.

A half dozen shirts, all colors, are in his fist, and his fist is half into his jacket. Louie stares right at me. Maybe his eyes open a little rounder. We play Statues for thirty seconds, and then he slowly tucks the shirts against his chest and zips his jacket. The whole time, I look right at him and he looks right at me, eyes pasted to opposite ends of an invisible tunnel. When he leaves, he passes close enough that I can see he needs to shave.

The rules say I am supposed to say, "Excuse me? Sir?" or some other line that will be his cue to pay for the stuff or run like hell, but I say nothing. I don't say word one.

A minute later these two maybe sixteen-year-old girls with big mall hair, spray-on jeans, cigarette breath, no brains and pregnancy in their near futures come in to fiddle with neon tube tops and giggle while they look sideways at me, the college boy, who they should only know is a twenty-three year-old flunky sophomore on the five-year plan. I give them my discount for two pairs of pink sweatpants that say, "Juicy" on the seat, but I know they will never come back. That's OK; what would I do with jailbait?

Later that week, I stand between two guys who argue over the best kind of weight belt. I am being careful to offer no opinion when at the edge of my vision, Louie, soft as a cat, pads into the store. Roger watches him, and Louie knows it. His hands are firmly in his pockets and he doesn't linger in any aisle. Incapable of a decision, the beefcakes choose both kinds of belt. They head for the cashier just as two Beamer-types snag Roger.

The floor of a busy retail store is a basketball court. The play is a pick and roll. Roger gives me the sign to pick up his man, Lightfingers Louie, we switch, and I am the point guard who will make sure Louie doesn't hurt us with a fast break.

The moment Louie sees that we are one-on-one, he stashes a pair of white high-tops into his jacket. A blur, and they are gone. Packages of sweatlets vanish. Sunglasses. Swim wear. Skiing goggles. I almost laugh out loud when I realize that Lightfingers Louie is not a fat guy, but that the belly I see in front of him is a gizmo he wears to carry stuff, a shoplifter's kangaroo pouch. His stare never leaves me as his hands work. His lashless eyes blink. That's all I see. Then, swift as a midnight ninja, he is gone.

At the same time he is being robbed of maybe a hundred dollars worth of junk, Roger the Success sells an $1,100 stationary bicycle guaranteed to make you sweat and go nowhere.

Commerce. Some comes in, less goes out.

Though he's made the best sale of the week, Roger is grim when he joins me. He asks if that weasel got away with anything, and I say I am sure the weasel did not. "Maybe he's just a lonely guy who shops everyday."

"Grow up, kid," he says, and leads me to the athletic shoe display. "Look at this," he says and waves his hand in an open space. "There was a pair of high-tops here this morning. You sell any high-tops?" Before I can answer Roger asks me again, "You sure you didn't see him grab anything?"

I tell him I saw nothing. He scratches his nose, looks at me a little funny, and then shakes his head. "How's your Dad these days?" he asks me.

"OK, I guess," I say. "He's in Europe with his new wife."

"You give him my regards when you see him," Roger says and heads to the stockroom he uses as an office, but just as he gets to the door he turns and asks, "You sure you saw nothing?"

I shrug my shoulders.

The weekend comes and goes. Wednesday, just before dinner, Louie appears. Roger is out grazing his nightly salad. Our cashier runs an emery board across her nails and Louie is loose among the fishing rods. His soft hands stroke the smooth fiberglass shafts.

I don't know what I think I will do, but when I turn into the aisle I see beside Louie is a kid, a boy maybe four or five years old who through neatly combed straw-yellow hair looks up at Louie. Louie squats beside the boy. He turns the crank of a reel, presses the chrome button that engages the drag, lets the kid turn the crank, and they both laugh when the reel whirs. When the boy notices me at the head of the aisle, he becomes solemn. His father stands.

"Can I help you?" I ask, and we start the performance.

Louie asks about the different rods. They whip in the air over his head. He mimes a cast or two, and I stand admiringly aside while he goes through the script, but we both know that anyone who steals T-shirts cannot afford this gear. Maybe he scopes out what he will shoplift tomorrow. But for now I am the salesman, he is the buyer, and the kid is awed by Daddy. I unlock the display case and present a tray of lures, bright gewgaws that sparkle with lacquer, beads and mirrors. Louie talks about trout and bass, about bottom fishing and surfcasting, and while I do not know diddley about this—and I think neither does Louie—the kid is taken in by our quiet fin-and-feathers camaraderie.

And then, like a shark among tuna, Roger descends. He slides between me and Louie and tells me to return to what I was doing, which was nothing at all. From the head of the aisle I watch, and though I cannot hear all the words, it is plain that Roger makes Louie look like the village idiot. His thin lips pursed, Roger shakes his head and protectively grabs the rods we've placed helter-skelter on the counter top and stands them neatly back in the wall rack. He swings the bar shut and snaps the padlock closed. Roger shakes his head again. With his palms up he asks, "How much were you preparing to spend?" When Louie cannot answer, the kid's face collapses.

While Roger humiliates Louie, I watch the kid. He suddenly jerks like he has stepped into hot water, his hand goes into his pocket, and even from the head of the aisle I swear I can see the kid sway and go pale.

They stand there a few more minutes. For pride's sake, Louie is not going to back down so quickly. The kid is trembling, and I wonder if he is subject to some sort of fit. He leans against his father, and with his free hand, the one not in his pocket, he tugs at his dad's pants leg. But Louie remains relaxed, then glances at his watchless wrist as though he has an appointment, seizes his son, and out they finally go.

"The next time that guy comes in here, you ask him if he

is buying, and if he says 'No,' you kick his ass out. If he won't leave, you call security."

"Come on, Roger."

"Come on, nothing. You think I'm that stupid? What would your father say if he knew what was going on?"

"Roger, my father doesn't care if I fall off the edge of the earth."

"You don't know your father at all. A father deserves more from a son."

I do not need to hear lectures about filial duty, not from Roger. This game I will not play. I say, "I'm history," and I hand him my plastic name tag.

Our cashier blows me a kiss as I leave Roger's Sporting Life. For a short while, I drift in the crowds, and then I realize Louie and his boy have to be outside, in open air, beneath sky.

I find Louie and the kid near the mall entrance on the aluminum benches that face the north parking lot. The kid is crying, and Louie's rat-white jacket is wrapped around the kid's hand.

I walk up behind them and say, "How you doing?"

Louie twists his head, sees who I am, returns his attention to his boy, and says, "We're OK."

"What's the matter with the kid?"

"Michael. He has a name. Michael."

"What's the matter with Michael?"

He unwraps Michael's hand. Blood streaks the jacket. In the center of Michael's palm is a feathered lure, the feather crushed and blood-soaked. Blood trickles steadily across his wrist and down his forearm to his elbow.

"The hook got into him. See it there? It looks worse than it is, but it must hurt like hell. You got a knife or scissors on you?"

I tell him I don't.

"Can you get one from the store?"

"I don't work there anymore."

Louie's blank, shallow eyes behind his rimless spectacles examine me a moment. "You'll be OK. Guys like you always get by," he says. "Give me a hand. Sit down. Hold Michael still. If he squirms, he'll make it worse."

I sit on the bench at Michael's feet. His head rests in his father's lap. I grab the boy at the knees. Through his rough jeans I can feel his supple muscles. He's a fine boy.

"The only way to get this out is to push the hook up and through the flesh. I saw it in a movie. Then I can bite off the nib, and the thing will slide out real easy. You ready for this, Michael?" He pushes Michael's hair from his damp forehead.

"It was a present," Michael says. "I took it for you."

The kid's blue eyes are wild. His lips are near white. His father lifts his hand to his lips and says, "This is going to hurt, Mikey," and then he pushes the hook farther into the boy's hand. Michael whimpers, and his legs stiffen in my grip, but he makes no other sound until he gasps when the hook's point penetrates his skin the second time. When the hook is exposed sufficiently, his father takes it between his teeth. It takes a minute. The whole time Michael is silent. When the metal snaps, I hear teeth click. He spits the bloody hook out, wipes his mouth with his wrist, sits erect, slides what is left of the metal backward through the boy's hand, and presses his jacket against the clean wound. The lure drops to the ground.

Michael hides his face against his father's abdomen. Free of pain, the little body shakes. I touch his legs. I feel him tremble.

Jody's Run

Tricia Walters

Jody's father went mute. His gray eyes glazed with stupor, then ignited with surprise and delight. His sudden smile infused every muscle of his face, passed through his cheeks, around his eyes, and crept up beyond his receding hairline. His fork floated motionless before his split-with-grinning lips. With a mix of fascination and horror, Jody watched a thick cascade of fettuccine alfredo wriggle like garter snakes as they dribbled from his fork to the edge of his plate to form a gummy heap of pasta on the tablecloth.

Granted, this was not Daddy's most distinguished moment, the man stunned as though he'd been smacked at the back of his head with a two-by-four. But then, as far as Jody knew, distinguished moments were rare in Daddy's plodding life. Short-legged and ordinary, Daddy's modest paunch fell loosely over a black belt scarred and cracked where the buckle had impressed itself into the leather cinched three inches tighter ten years ago, half of Jody's lifetime. No, distinction was not prominent on Cy Phillips' resumé.

Not for lack of Jody's effort, either. She'd contributed more than any good daughter's expected quota of new belts, she'd presented miles of patterned ties, and one desperate Father's Day she'd gone so far as to gift-wrap a pair of two-inch-wide purple and green paisley suspenders. It would have made more sense to give a wallet to a fish.

Cy Phillips considered argyle socks an unwarranted, unacceptably wild adventure. He avoided risk and, as far as Jody knew, had never committed an act of impulse. So when Daddy gently placed his utensil beside his plate, lifted his linen napkin to wipe his chin clean, and said, "You see that woman over there? In the black and white suit? I haven't seen her in fifteen, maybe sixteen years. Look at her; you'd never guess she once starred in the circus," Jody wondered which aliens had abducted her father and replaced him with this grinning clone.

Daddy knew a circus star?

Jody turned to see, but through the jungle of ferns and coleus saw only stained ceiling beams, aproned waitresses, sweating silver wine buckets, and the shimmering doubled glow of candles reflected in globes of glass. Daddy's exotic New York restaurants were always located down or up a flight of stairs, anywhere but street-level. They were places where people whispered to each other before they came to impor-tant, often scandalous, decisions; they were places a girl like Jody could by dim light safely spill her humiliating soft drink into the soil of something that grew.

As Jody twisted in her seat, her elbow brushed the top of her chicken tarragon, adding yet another shapeless stain to her gray Champion sweatshirt, already crusted with five colors of poster paint, traces of a set design project gone awry. Simultaneously, a red-jacketed waiter stepped to his left, allowing Jody her first glimpse of the Circus Gorgon that cast Professor Cy open-mouthed into stone.

The woman sipped what had to be Chardonnay and listened intently to the man across the table from her. Gems—nothing gaudy—decorated her neck and fingers. Her neat black hair was short, practically boyish, the kind you could shower, towel dry, and forget as you dashed barefoot to the Paris Opera, your shoes only on your feet when you made it into the Mercedes limo where you defied class differences and uncaringly sat beside your chauffeur to commandeer the driver's rearview mirror to apply your crimson lipstick—Cherries in the Snow.

But despite her short hair, no one had ever mistaken this woman for a boy. It was not so much her perfect figure as the way she carried herself, the exquisite tilt of her wrist as she lifted her wine glass, the engaging angle of her chin, the fine facial bones beneath skin luminous as a Lladró figurine. The woman's simple sleeveless suit might have been by Chanel. It had to be by Chanel. Nothing else ever looked that good. But it wasn't quite Chanel. Something was amiss. What shoes were beneath the table? Louis Vuitton? Manolo Blahnik? Ferragamo?

If God had chosen to flip the room upside down, the one-time trapeze flyer in black and cream would not only land on her delicate feet, she would politely demand of the Lord a detailed explanation for His eccentric behavior.

Jody felt her youth, a stone on her chest.

At that precise moment, the woman made eye contact with Jody. It was too late to sink below the table. Remembering the glance years later, Jody felt that something without a name, some shared connection strong as steel bridge cable passed along that line of sight. But in the restaurant, at the moment when she was twenty years old and dining with her father, the flustered girl only struggled to avert her glance. She'd never learn a name for what she felt. It remained another mystery.

Then predictable Cy fooled her for the second time in mere minutes. Ordinarily world-class shy, Olympic Silver for Freestyle Antisocial Behavior (the Gold to Greta Garbo), that same Cy Phillips leapt from his seat and tugged at his daughter so swiftly that she had no chance to release the Diet Pepsi with a twist of lime they'd served unasked as a mocktail to the underage kid.

At her table, the circus star's slim hand folded gently about Daddy's. "Cy, it's been much too long." Her speech was precisely cultured. When had Public Speaking made the curriculum at Clown College? Did circus stars have sultry, trained voices, raspy as Jacqueline Onassis's? True, this woman's voice was rougher and at least an octave higher. She had absolutely jade green eyes. The palest pink nail polish, daringly perfect with black and cream. Maybe it was Chanel. Silk, mostly. Lace, the real stuff. This woman had never known a synthetic fabric.

"Is this . . . My God, you must be Jody."

Wiggling her fingers in a frenzy of greeting, Jody tried simultaneously to lock her hands behind her back, an impossible posture aggravated by the slippery glass in her left hand. The stuff soaked her wrist and the cuff of her sweatshirt. Surely, the waiter who'd adorned her drink with a red-striped straw needed killing; the straw had tiny accordion folds for easy bending, and so it looked like the windsock at a mouse airport. Jody held her glass in front of her, an out-of-pencils blind beggar desperate to sell a bent straw, unable to take the woman's proffered hand.

When had her life become this pathetic? She wondered if Daddy was constitutionally incapable of alerting her to the appropriate garb for the places he took her. It was not as though she did not have an appropriate dress. Her closet was filled with the sensible outfits in subdued colors that Daddy's wife sent to Jody, all a roomy size 6. Okay, maybe not Chanel; not even Donna Karan, but Jody knew the basics of couture well enough to know it when she saw it. Only her wallet loved Wal-Mart. Every man and woman around her wore a suit; Jody cleverly wore rags, bra-less in shapeless razor-slit clothes. Hopeless in Birkenstock sandals and gray sweatsocks, at least with a warning from Daddy, she might have tied back and brushed her hair, which, unattended, looked as though it was the nest for small furry things that spent winters curled in hibernation behind her ears.

And the woman in front of them? Daddy's circus star? Well, she was a swirl of diamonds and emeralds on a field of sultry black and cream white. Up close, Jody saw her error: the woman's eyes were not jade green, rather, her eyes matched her emeralds. *Naturellement.* The look was unmistakably understated, classic without being dated. It could be Chanel, but it wasn't.

"Jody, this is . . ."

"My name is Tricia Walters."

Tricia Walters then introduced her silent friend. He half rose from the booth to extend his hand first to Cy and then to Jody. His piqué shirt was white on white. His fingernails contained perfect half-moon cuticles covered with clear polish. He was much older than Tricia Walters, at least sixty. Older than even Daddy. The lines at Tricia Walters's eyes weren't deep; nevertheless, the skin at her throat was drum tight without that look of shrink-wrap, No nip and tuck had ever surgically augmented her appearance. She wasn't forty.

She asked Daddy why he'd returned to New York this time.

Daddy said, "The usual. A conference. Academic stuff. I am at the Sheraton."

The usual? The conference was a complete fabrication, Jody knew but said nothing. Cy Phillips was in town to check on his only child, his daughter. "And Jody here is in her sophomore year at Columbia." Daddy was incapable of simply admitting that he missed his daughter, and that missing her was reason enough for a journey from the Midwest.

The man in the ridiculously elegant shirt said, "Columbia?" When he moved, his gray suit jacket parted long enough for Jody to see the blue monogram embroidered on his shirt pocket. His cufflinks were set with amethysts. "Isn't that a college for men?"

"Only the more strident women stay separate at Barnard," Jody said and felt ridiculous when the older man lifted his baleful eyes to her. What cave had he been in for the past decade? "I go to Columbia."

"How do you find college?" Tricia Walters asked.

"Dean's List," her father quickly lied.

Tricia Walters's smile indicated that she knew all about Daddy's propensity to speak for other people. The woman's teeth were even and white, just asymmetrical enough to prove they had never been capped.

Little questions were asked and vaguely answered. Tricia Walters had knocked around and then had come to rest. Here and there. This and that.

"I'd heard," Daddy said.

Daddy had settled in Minneapolis, mourned the passing of Jody's mother, and remarried.

"I'd heard," Tricia Walters said.

Now what was this? They heard? How? When? As far as Jody knew, telepathy didn't run in the Phillips family. When had Daddy turned psychic?

Tricia Walters said, "It's a treat seeing you, Cy. You look the same."

Daddy laughed.

She blinked and the eyes became smoky. "Don't laugh, Cy. You know I never kid. You look terrific."

Daddy, a man who liked to laugh, stopped laughing. Their hands finally parted.

Jody and her father retreated to their table. Over congealing Alfredo sauce and cold chicken tarragon, Jody asked, "When did I make Dean's List?"

"It was just something to say. Why make a big deal out of it?"

"It is a big deal. When you try to make me something I am not, it makes me feel bad about being what I am."

"Are we going to go through this again? Let's just finish lunch."

"I work like a coolie just to scrape by. I'd have been happier at the community college in Saint Paul. Much happier."

It never hurt to dispense mild guilt, even if it meant resorting to a mild lie. She adored New York City and would have been miserable in St. Paul, but Daddy's visits often left hard currency in their wake; a tiny falsehood was an investment that often brought dividends.

She'd been admitted to Columbia after a less than illustrious high school career, some ridiculously elevated college board scores that could only have been the result of a power surge on the computer as it scanned answer sheets, and an old-boy network telephone call from Daddy to an assistant dean of admissions.

Buttered string beans and soft almonds rolled around her tongue. "So, who is Tricia Walters?" she asked.

"You're being careful? When you run? Are you still doing that?"

"Fifteen, maybe twenty miles a week. It works off the jelly donuts and pizza. Did you ever try pizza with french fries? Totally amazing." She seized a hot rye roll from the bread basket, shifted her weight, and thrust it into her pocket.

"Why not go out for track?"

"Give me a break, Daddy. Me? The words *Jody* and *team* have never been in the same sentence."

Daddy shrugged. "Well, I wish you'd run indoors. New York isn't Minnesota. I worry about you. So does Sarah."

Sarah, her stepmother, never traveled with Daddy when he visited Jody. "This is America. I don't need a passport to run in a public park. Besides, everyone knows that bad things only happen to people who worry about them." She sipped the remains of her drink until the straw crackled. "Look, I run with a group of people," she lied. "I'm okay, Daddy."

With a three-tine fork, Jody peeled the white flesh of chicken from a breastbone. When she looked up, her father's gray eyes had glazed like a Krispy Kreme again. Tricia Walters and her companion hovered over them.

"Jody," the woman said. She tucked a curl of her black hair behind her ear. The green, double-0 rated eyes had gone ocean deep again. Weightless as a butterfly, her jeweled hand lighted on Jody's shoulder, then withdrew from her beaded purse a cocktail napkin on which she'd written a telephone number. Jody braved a quick glance to the floor. Manolo Blahnik?

No, too uncomfortable, but those were Ferragamo. No doubt about it. You'd think she'd have stayed with Chanel down to her feet, but those were those wonderful black Ferragamo three-inch heels. Maybe size 4. Jody wore a 7. She had feet like Donald Duck.

The woman in black and cream and emeralds and diamonds and Ferragamo boots smiled at her. Then she bent close and whispered, "You're staring. The suit is Bottega Veneta. The new winter line. Marvelous, isn't it?" She straightened up and said, "I'd appreciate it if you'd call me if you need any kind of assistance."

Jody flushed pink. Had she been that obvious? At least she'd been half right: it wasn't Chanel.

Daddy said, "Jody can take care of herself."

What was this? Minutes ago, she was incapable of crossing Broadway to Morningside Park without an armed escort, and now, as far as Tricia Walters was to know, Jody had the resources of a pioneer woman. She'd have to examine Bottega Veneta online, the entire collection. Subdued understated classic lines. God. How had it gotten by her?

"Cy, no offense and with love and respect, I was talking to Jody." Tricia Walters bent and actually chucked Daddy's chin, a gesture so surprising and intimate it nearly made Jody laugh, something she had not allowed herself to do in public for years. Daddy grinned like a tickled infant. "You needn't be in trouble, Jody. We should . . . know each other." Tricia Walters wrote hastily on a cocktail napkin.

Jody placed the napkin beside her plate.

Tricia Walters turned to Daddy. "Take care of yourself, Cy," she said, seemed to almost bend to kiss him, and then Jody watched the large man and Tricia Walters leave. The circus star in high couture moved like a feral cat used to three-inch heels. At the door, she discreetly pressed money into the maître d's hand, then pulled on elbow length white gloves while she waited for her companion to hold her coat.

"Who is she?"

"One of my former students. That's all."

That made no sense for a woman who'd chucked him under the chin. So Jody said, "She must have known Mother. From the time when we were a family in New York. That's why she knows my name, isn't it? From when I was a baby."

"I guess." And then Daddy did something extraordinary. He looked at his watch and then gestured to the waiter. Daddy hurried? "Trish never met your mother."

"*Trish?*"

"Let's skip dessert."

Jody and Cy Phillips always ordered dessert, usually something with chocolate sauce and raspberries; they just never ate it. With two forks, they picked, and then took it with them sealed in Styrofoam. Jody's job was to discard it days later, and, if her father asked, report that she'd enjoyed every last morsel.

"Do you suppose she was serious? About me calling her. What would I say?"

"Where is that guy?" Daddy's fingers drummed the tablecloth. "I have to get you back uptown. I have a meeting at three."

Cy Phillips impatient? Store canned goods. Buy shotguns. Telegraph Chicken Little: the sky was falling.

"Just put me in a taxi," she said, "Save yourself some time."

He eagerly nodded.

Their waiter placed the check on the table. Without verifying the total, Daddy slapped a credit card on top of the leatherette holder, then looked into the folds of his wallet, retrieved his credit card, and replaced it with five twenty dollar bills.

Cash? Daddy was in so much of a hurry that he was laying out cash! Unheard of—little green coupons with the portraits of the presidents!

Halfway to the door, Jody remembered the cocktail napkin. She charged back to the table just in time to rescue it from a Puerto Rican busboy. The telephone number had been written with a fountain pen. The black ink bled into the porous paper, delicate as a rose petal.

Bent into the cold wind, they walked from Madison to Park Avenue. Her father gave her fifty dollars. No doubt about it, Daddy was hemorrhaging money. "Take cab fare from that." He stepped off the curbstone, his arm in the air, staring into the flow of uptown traffic like Columbus peering into an east wind.

Into her mind and out of her mouth, Jody said, "She's a call girl, right?"

"Who?"

"Your former student. Tricia Walters. All those gems, the clothes, God did you see her shoes? Her shoes could pay my tuition, Daddy! And that fat man. She's a call girl. Right? A call girl."

"Don't be ridiculous. Last I heard she made her own fortune. She's in some artsy-fartsy business. I don't know all the details."

Last he'd heard? When had he heard? How?

"Well, she's pretty enough to be a call girl," Jody muttered and wondered if Tricia Walters could be a madam. She was a little old to be a call girl. Maybe she'd graduated.

A taxi braked beside them. Daddy opened the door and practically shoved Jody in. "Pretty? Yes, I suppose she is pretty. Give us a kiss good-bye." He bent forward. The wind tousled his thinning hair. His gray eyes were tired and distracted, runny with cold. She kissed her father's cheek. Jody waved, and realized that she still held the cocktail napkin in her hand.

Daddy slammed the door.

Shouting at the Pakistani driver to stop, she lunged to the window and rolled it open. "Do you want this?" she shouted and held the fluttering napkin out to him.

His gloved hand swiped at the base of his nose, he thrust his clenched fists into his jacket pockets, and his shoulders rose. "No. I don't want it. Absolutely don't want it."

Truth, a rose, blossomed before her. "You were lovers," she blurted out.

Daddy's rheumy gray eyes snagged her. "Boy, Jo, you are some piece of work," he said, and Daddy's hand slammed flat on the taxi's hard metal roof, bang!

The cab lurched and Jody fell back against the vinyl seat. Through the open window, cold air and the noise of the city washed over her as she realized he'd mentioned his hotel. I'm at the Sheraton.

Did Daddy hurry on the chance Tricia Walters would find him?

Words cold-lit as fireflies flitted through Jody's head. Beautiful words. Marvelous words. Words she had never associated with her father, Casual Cy. Paramour. Tryst. Rendezvous. There was more here than sordid scandal—there was Romance.

She carefully folded the napkin and slid it in her pocket beside the roll. Meeting Tricia Walters would beat all hollow fraternity boys who wanted to read poetry naked.

Daddy would not need to know. Who could say? Perhaps Tricia Walters and Mother once met. Daddy would not have needed to know.

Courageous, competent women did such things; men never needed to know.

Nearly two years in New York City, and she'd finally met a woman who might know what Jody needed to learn: the confidence, self-possession, and certainty opened only to those who willingly stare unflinchingly into the unadorned face of their own motives.

This Tricia Walters could not possibly be like Jody's mother. Not at all like that craven bitch.

Jody

Mother died the clear April afternoon her unimpeded car took flight off a two-lane blacktop Minnesota road into a wall of unyielding pine trees. Suicide? Recklessness? Maybe she'd swerved to avoid a deer. There were no skid marks. Her death was inexplicable. Jody had been four.

Mother's only legacy was Jody's anger and fuzzy memories of sheets that smelled of Clorox, blankets warm from the dryer, a soft voice, a sapphire-blue sequined dress, and an aroma Jody thought special until at twelve she disgustedly confirmed was nothing more exotic than Johnson's Baby Powder. That had seemed Mother's final betrayal.

Jody had been on her own since forever. Everything she knew that was worth knowing, she had taught herself. A girl's education was a chancy proposition, one that only marginally occurred in a classroom, and, for a girl with no mother, what she knew and what she did not came down to a roll of the dice.

During her adolescence, in Jody's suburb of St. Paul, the color of spring lawns was a subject of endless comment, rabid raccoons were deemed a threat to the general welfare, and wagering nickels on the number of insects electrocuted in a fifteen-minute interval could pass an otherwise dull July night. In her suburb of St. Paul, as they did everywhere, boys twisted and sweated alone in their sheets, but in Jody's suburb of St. Paul their most fevered dreams were of four barrel carburetion, pin-striping, nitro fuel, titanium suspension systems, and windshields tinted so dark a highway patrolman with his nose against the glass would still not see a driver flash the finger. Girls were less essential than a cam rod, as interchangeable as bucket seats, and only marginally preferred to a chrome hood ornament.

Confronted by such endless opportunities for cultivating self-esteem, Jody adopted a studied posture of complete indifference. Her attitude was communicated by slowly chewing gum, applying black mascara as if with a trowel, and rolling her eyes at the approach of any and all authority figures. She perfected a sigh of impatience that infuriated teachers, librarians, and shopping mall rent-a-cops, and she could pronounce the word *God* as though it had two syllables, as in the phrase, "Well, Guhh-oddd, we were only standing here," or "Guhh-oddd, we were hardly talking." She drove every adult she knew wild, every adult except Daddy the Great Historian, who at each new outrage—louder music, dog collars, a pierced nostril, her threat to have her back tattooed with a tramp stamp—sucked on his meerschaum pipe and murmured, "*C'est la dada*," a French phrase that as far as Jody could ascertain meant, "I am the Daddy."

But on the battered desk in her room, he deposited books: poetry, history, political science, obscure novels translated from German, French, or Russian, and from time to time he'd leave a magazine opened to an article he thought interesting. He never knew which she read and which she ignored because, if he'd asked, she'd have denied having touched the stuff. In fact, she read them all, even the ones she hardly understood, pushing obsessively to the final page of every volume. When Daddy obtained a pass for her to use the Macalester College library, she accepted it without comment, and went without him ever knowing. The exhibit on haute couture in 1950s Paris had changed her life.

Some girls puked, some cut their flesh, some huffed airplane glue. Jody's secret vice was to hold a flashlight with her chin and read at night beneath the tent of her blanket until when her eyeballs rolled they felt like they were set in sandpaper.

Fortunately, the consequent black circles under her eyes proved something of a status symbol, a complement to the black eyeliner that made Jody appear "wasted," high praise from fifteen-year-old dopers and gear heads eager to emulate heroin chic. Jody colored her hair from yellow to blue to green and back to yellow, teased her bangs, and then sprouted banana curls that drooped like jungle vines over her shoulders, always bare except for a ratty bra strap forever visible because she'd excised the collars of all her sweatshirts with pinking sheers. In a bathtub of cold water, she wore jeans that shrank to the precise contours of her spreading hips and knobby ass. She snapped gum, smoked Marlboro when she was out of Daddy's range, and whispered with girl friends about the finer aspects of applying makeup, beer can rollers, and delivering a cosmically effective blow-job despite rubber bands, hooks, plates, steel, tin, and the other impediments of orthodonture. No, the significant parts of a girl's education never occur in a classroom.

Take Bobby Williams, for example. They had been fourteen together, and he was not half as smart as she, which made him perfect. Bobby sold a little dope that he filched from his brother, and he smoked a lot more. She adored his bravado, confusing it with the toughness that her circle commonly understood to be available exclusively to men.

Jody and Bobby drank beer and smoked blunts in Dorsey's Field, a wilderness of weeds, rocks, and shattered glass that overlooked the cemetery where Mother rested. On his MoPed, her arms encircled Bobby's waist, her wrists against the hard knots of muscles just above his belt, her still not fully formed breasts flattened against his bony back. He was sweet, and since he was not terribly bright, she easily felt herself to be his equal.

So one night at Dorsey's Field, Bobby Williams was surprised more than a little when Jody withdrew a small blanket from her backpack, but he was knocked out when he learned just what his girlfriend had in mind. His butt was hard as September apples. The lovers were so skinny, their bones rubbed. He was on her and off before she was sure they'd done anything right.

"Now you'll love me," she whispered to him while he fumbled for a cigarette in his jeans pocket.

He sat up. "What are you? Crazy?"

But they worked at it. Bobby improved, if just a little. She was bold enough to tell him what to do, and when he bragged to a few people about what was going on, she almost forgave him as she endured the whispering, giggling, rolled eyes and the word "slut" scrawled on her books. Daddy got wind of what was going on, seemed unperturbed, checked if she had taken precautions, and said to her that her peers hated her for having courage. Then he lighted a pipe, took her for icecream, and recommended that she slow down.

God, how could anyone deal with a father like that?

Her junior year, Jody was forced to take a drama class. It was that or computers, and everyone knew a girl in a computer class was doomed to acne. The new drama teacher, Mr. Bledsoe, couldn't have been more than twenty-five, had a blond beard and wore tweed jackets, forest green or black turtleneck shirts, tan slacks, and beat up running shoes. Bledsoe explained Oedipus's agony and the exquisite depths of Hamlet's despair. Sitting in the back of Bledsoe's classroom, Jody saw how a great heart, a vast soul, and a significant life required the great good luck of being miserable. Why bruise her thighs on Wham-Bam Williams? Why squander her youth on a guy whose highest ambition was to learn to turn a lathe? Whatever it meant to be an existential hero, she would find one.

Rumor had it that Mr. Bledsoe boffed Janet Whitman in the school's darkroom. Janet, the source of the rumor, considered herself an advanced young woman. Who'd say otherwise: her poetry appeared regularly in *The Northway*. Janet confided to a friend that Bledsoe wore sheer royal blue nylon bikini briefs, a bit of intelligence that in mere hours caused considerable hyperventilation among the high school literati, professional virgins, every one.

Jody, however, put no credence in the rumor. By now a loner who'd shed cigarettes and the mall crowd, Jody kept her own councils and studied this Bledsoe. Having shared laundry duty with Daddy from when she was ten, and having grown familiar with sorry-ass Bobby's red boxer trunks pulled visibly above the waist of his cargo pants, she knew a few things about men's drawers. Bledsoe, she was sure, wore plain briefs. Hanes, maybe. Jockey, perhaps. You could tell by the fabric line. Maybe they were black. Tidy-whities, most likely. They might even have been royal blue, but for damned certain they were cotton. If he mixed darks and lights, which Daddy always did, maybe they were pink. They sure weren't any sheer nylon banana hammocks.

Janet Whitman might write awesome rhyming poems about weeping clouds and flowers that struggled for the sun, symbolic proof that Beauty was nurtured by Nature's grief, but when it came to men's undies, the girl knew bubblefuck.

Suffering a faint tingle of lust, Jody realized that to become the intellectual equal of a man like Bledsoe would require effort. Jody mentioned to her father that she might, after all, be interested in attending college. Her grades inched upward. She earned her first A. In Drama.

Columbia granted her provisional acceptance. She spent a year in Morningside Heights with her legs closed and her mouth shut, two habits that allowed her to listen and learn, but she returned home with the object of informing Daddy that despite her best effort, College was not for her. Her classmates were too smart, her teachers too demanding, and she had no clue, none, as to what she was doing there.

So that summer, after a year of humiliation, months before she met Tricia Walters, she returned home to a place she'd never been, Daddy's new gentleman's farm. He grew nothing more complicated than untended hay, already contracted to be cut by a neighbor, Bud Johnson.

Daddy and his new wife, Sarah, had moved from the city to a real farmhouse, a rickety affair set between two trees on a low hill overlooking what Daddy said was sixty-five acres. At the hill's base was a pond with water that remained clear.

Of the three second-floor guest rooms, Jody chose the room with the white iron daybed. Through the big square windows, framed by the twin trees, she could see the dirt road that ran by their land climb a green hill and curl away to the horizon. In the day's heat, Jody's white damask curtains hung limp; in the cooler night, those curtains stirred gently.

Jody was sure she'd go mad from boredom; Daddy would not allow her to get a job. His Jody-Girl did not need to work, so one day when she and Sarah visited a mall, to amuse herself, she purchased running shoes. How could Daddy object to healthful exercise?

She took to running. They were cheap shoes, but she got good at it, became antsy when she neglected to run for more than a day or two, and when she achieved two miles per day, the sport crept to the center of her existence. She charged a pair of better Nikes to Daddy's card and began running in the mornings to avoid the worst of the heat. The impact of her foot striking the earth traveled from the ground up her legs to her pelvis, but after her first mile she no longer felt the ground beneath her. A three-mile run became effortless. Her feet navigated independently, her thighs churned, her mind a passenger afloat in her skull. Dew soaked through the felt toe box of her shoes, her breath inflated her chest, her skin ran so freely with sweat that her shirt clung to her, a second skin. Wearily stepping up to the farmhouse porch, she'd pinch the material at her belly, pull it forward in a conic tent, release it, and feel it slap satisfyingly against her flat stomach.

She began running twice each day, once in the morning and then later toward the evening with no intention of doing more than five miles for a total, until she realized she was doing seven. Until she treated herself to a running bra, her T-shirt so chafed her nipples that they bled. Her calves thickened; her skin browned; there was space in the seat of her jeans. She marveled at the sinew of her own thighs.

Some mornings she soared past a pasture where a black horse grazed. Seeing her, the stallion's graceful long neck would lift its great head, he'd examine her with a rolling, liquid eye, and, if he felt like it, which was frequent, he'd gallop easily on his side of the fence beside her. She'd hear the rush of the stallion's breath, and she would run to the rhythm of the animal's hooves.

Much to Sarah's disapproval, Jody allowed hair to grow in her armpits. After showering in the morning, she stood before the long bathroom mirror, her arms bent behind her head, examining the delicate tufts of what she could only think of as fur. It made her feel untamed, slightly wild, and therefore less disruptive of the landscape through which she darted every day. She went to bed at darkness and rose at first light. The moon, stars, sun and the planet's rotation regulated her life. When she missed a period, she was unconcerned; it was from running. No other cause was possible, not for the Lone Prisoner of the Prairie.

In mid-August, Daddy and his wife rewarded themselves with a two-week vacation. Jody refused to be parked with friends or neighbors, all strangers to her.

Her first night alone, she wondered if she'd made a mistake. Jody strained her ears against the numbing quiet of the country until she heard crickets and cicada and the night became alive. The empty farmhouse grew animate with groans and sighs. Shadows became quick. Jody slept with an old radio murmuring by her head. Sweating, her heart pounding, she awakened twice, the second time shouting, "Who's there?"

On the hottest nights, she walked through air thick with insects to the pond. Beneath the dome of the night sky, she felt safer. It was easy for her to step from her shorts and t-shirt, leaving her clothes in a warm, dark pile of shadow. She parted the thick reeds that grew at the pond's edge and slipped into water that by moonlight shimmered like a droplet of mercury in a cupped palm of earth. She paddled gently to the pond's center, her long arms just barely rippling the glassy moonlit surface into black wavelets that fled from her to the shore. Her toes sank in soft bottom mud. On shore, moonlight shone on her wet flesh. When she shook her head, water droplets cast from her hair caught the light and fell like cold sparks of silver flame.

She feared only thunderstorms. She had since she was a child, hiding in closets if Daddy was not home to comfort her, enduring the worst face-down beneath a poplin blanket with a pillow crushed tightly over her ears. The unrestrained power terrified her. Inches of rain could fall in minutes, followed by hail that sounded like a cascade of pennies on a tin roof. On the northern plains, thunder might shake the land, and a wind that slid off the east face of the Rockies roared like an unimpeded freight train accelerating across a thousand miles of open prairie before colliding with rattling panes of glass in her flimsy windows.

A week after Daddy and Sarah left, Jody was awakened by a tractor chattering to life. When Jody parted the green-checkered curtains at the kitchen window and peered out, she saw wide, wet tracks of freshly cut grass like long wounds on the land. The tractor pulled the swather the length of the field, circled, and then carefully returned close beside the path it had just run. It was Mr. Johnson, their neighbor, the man who'd contracted for Daddy's hay.

Jody leaned against the door. She chewed dry rye toast and drank decaffeinated coffee. Then she stretched her hamstrings by lifting her ankles to the balustrade and ran for an hour. Jody no longer measured distance. It was time on her feet that mattered. Along her route, the air smelled newly green.

For two days, the cut grass lay drying in the sun, and then Mr. Johnson towed a baler through the field, a great flat machine with a broad mouth and blades for teeth. Grass was ingested, and rectangular bales the size of steamer trunks passed up the long neck to be spat onto the ground.

In three days, the bales dried yellow. That third day, the sky was cloudless and the low sun a burning gold coin when in early morning Jody watched four blond, tow-headed high school boys trot after Mr. Johnson's tractor as it towed a hay-rick. They slowly moved across the land, two boys on the rick stacking; two on the ground lifting and heaving bales to the boys who rode.

Jody decided not to run but retrieved a book from the house's dark interior. She placed the book in her lap while she watched the boys from the porch's shade. She did not even look at the title.

At lunch, Mr. Johnson and the boys pulled up beside Daddy's empty, gray barn. Jody reclined on a white Saratoga chair. Mr. Johnson waved to her, then slowly ambled over to ask how she'd been doing, what with her Daddy having asked him to keep a lookout for her. She took off her sunglasses to talk and told him she was doing fine. She offered him and the boys lemonade, which Mr. Johnson declined. Crossed at the ankles, she propped her bare legs on the porch railing.

The boys sprawled on the ground with their legs before them, leaning back on their bent wrists, shirtless on the ground in the shade of one of the trees where they ate their lunches and drank water from a rubber hose. Their arms and hairless chests seemed golden as the sun shone on their sweat, their biceps spotted by shreds of grass, bandanas tied at their foreheads. Jody pretended to read. They had narrow hips, broad shoulders, and the muscles in their arms were twisted as rope.

They went behind the barn to pee, and, after they ate, they pulled their shirts back on and propped a motorized endless belt from the ground to the barn loft. Mr. Johnson cursed the elevator's motor for a time, tugging at the starting cord. Then the air filled with the sweet smell of the little engine's blue exhaust.

"Stack right to the roof," Mr. Johnson called, and Jody imagined the boys bending and lifting, their skin running with sweat and their voices rough with dust in the close heat.

When they were through, they rinsed their faces, hands, and necks with water from the running hose. Mr. Johnson came close to say that he and Mrs. Johnson would be pleased if she felt like joining them sometime for a meal, but Jody said she was doing just fine.

"Mrs. Johnson sees you run sometimes," he added. "In her opinion, a girl can have too much muscle." He stood back and looked at her as he would look at livestock. She wore pink nylon running shorts and a white T-shirt, her stomach hard. "You look fine to me," he added, turned, then spun to whisper that if she had heard any of the boys' remarks about her, she should pay no mind. "They don't mean no harm by it," he explained. "Just healthy boys."

The healthy boys unfurled Deere hats from their back pockets and soaked them with water before they left. It was near dinner, and she watched them pull their heads through their shirts, hearing them joke about how they had grass and chiggers in places where they did not know they had places.

Clouds accumulated shortly after they were gone. The high heat of the day had broken. As the clouds mounted, Jody allowed herself to think about the boys, those shining, golden boys. Those good boys. Those good shining boys who made dirty remarks about her but meant nothing by it.

The sun tinted pink the bottoms of great thunderheads piling higher at the western horizon. Air stirred. Jody went inside when her arms raised gooseflesh. Though it was hours before sunset, the last light outside transmuted from pink to red to violet. She toed off her Tretorn tennis shoes and pulled her T-shirt over her head. In the farmhouse's dim interior, she fell back on the sofa and thought a little more about the boys. Then she touched herself until she trembled just a little, and then she drifted into a dreamless sleep.

A crack of thunder awakened her. She bolted upright, became disoriented, and to clear her mind wandered to the kitchen where she sat on a hard wooden chair, her breath shallow and rapid as she waited for the wail of a tornado siren. The electric lights yellowed and flickered. Wind like flood waters eddied and clutched at the house. The windows rattled. Through her bare feet, beneath the cold linoleum, she felt the floor shake.

She could not simply wait for disaster. She heard no siren, but Jody knew what was what.

In bra and running shorts, Jody stood in the farmhouse doorway. It should have been night, but the sky glowed ominous green and purple. By a lightning flash, she saw the twin oaks yield to the storm, bend, then snap erect before bowing again, their leaves brushing the earth. Lightning splashed shadows across the lawn. Hail briefly pelted the porch and lay like a carpet of melting rhinestones about her feet.

She should stay near the cellar, but instead Jody moved from the roofed porch's shelter out to the yard, unwilling to consider danger from lightning. Her bare feet sank in mud. Rain washed wisps of hay blown onto her hair and shoulders, leaving her chilled. The wind drove water like needles into her back and belly. To still her rising panic, she inhaled, filling chest with the aroma of wet firewood stacked by the house. She raised her arms to the storm, and icy water flowed down her bare thighs as wind grabbed at the bare backs of her legs. Nothing was between her and the weather except an old bra, her pink running shorts, and the cotton bikini panties she wore beneath.

She shivered and pushed open the small gate and walked to the center of the ruler-straight road that fronted the house.

Face into the wind, she shouted wordlessly. Her hands clenched to fists. She matched the storm's fury, shouted until she heard only herself.

And then she ran, all she knew to do.

Slick with water, her muscled thighs brushed against each other with a smoothness impossible if she had been clothed. Without breaking stride, she shed her bra, dropping it into the darkness, and felt the same oiled freedom as her arms brushed frictionless along her ribs.

She ran through a landscape scoured by wind. She ran barefoot, ignoring the pain. The rain-softened earth yielded easily, and her feet touched ground so briefly she was sure she flew, held perfectly evenly between the earth and sky, floating like an unborn child. Running topless in the night, all she could know was her body and its effort—muscles, lungs, heart and blood. When lightning flashed, the flat land seemed color-bled and alien. Her legs vaulted her over ditches gurgling with black water. She heard the beat of a horse's hooves before her and to the right, and by a flash of lightning saw her stallion's eye, red and rolling with bestial panic, and then she left the black horse in darkness behind her.

She ran and ran and ran until the storm abated.

Days later, Daddy and Sarah returned with sweatshirts and chocolates from San Francisco. Jody thought of how she'd thought to tell Daddy she needed to leave school, but instead she announced she was returning early to New York.

Her father said, "Nonsense," and waved his hand. "You've got two weeks more of vacation. What could my Jody-Girl do in New York City?"

"I'll think of something," she said.

The Wheel of Death

That following November, after a week searching for the courage she'd need and hours of inspecting the website for Bottega Veneta, Jody called the number on the cocktail napkin. The male voice that answered had just the slightest hint of a British accent. "Sultana Jewelry." Jody hung up.

Sultana had no website, but the Yellow Pages told her that Sultana Jewelry was headquartered on Hudson Street. She ripped the page from the book. Daddy had already departed the Sheraton and fled to the safety of Minnesota and a traditional Thanksgiving with Sarah. Had Daddy and Tricia connected?

That afternoon, with no appointment, Jody planned to pop in boldly on Tricia Walters, the jewelry designer and circus star who had slept with Daddy just as Jody had come into the world. Jody wanted the advantage of surprise, though she was fairly sure no one had ever maintained a lasting advantage over Tricia Walters by so cheap a trick. The idea was laughable, but surely she could do better than the hopeless goon-child she had been in the restaurant with Daddy.

She applied a face to seem worldly, but mascara made her look like a vampire, blush made her look like a kewpie doll, and eye shadow made her look like a badly painted corpse, so she scrubbed her face, added just a touch of coral color to her lips, and, after emptying her bureau and closet discovered she had no clothing that did not make her look like Rebecca going for broke on an escape from Sunnybrook Farm. She seized Daddy's emergency credit card. If this did not qualify as an emergency, nothing ever would.

Mad with need, she took a bus to Bloomingdale's where she bought a yellow silk dress and black patent leather belt, yellow knit top, black heels, black sweater, black bag, yellow knit beret. Running had reduced her to size 4. She stuffed her street clothes into a shopping bag and dropped it into garbage can on 3rd Avenue.

Yellow and black: she felt like a hornet.

She raised an arm into the air. Though rain threatened and cabs should have been scarce, three taxis nearly collided getting to her. That told her what she needed to know—the outfit worked

At Sultana, she intimidated a receptionist who was more than a little astonished when Ms. Walters ordered via intercom. "Cancel my afternoon."

Tricia Walters's corner office looked north over Hudson Street. In these final days of November, by 3:30, it was neither day nor night. Auto headlamps and towering buildings beyond the tinted glass seemed flat. The opalescent sky dripped cranky rain. An isolated, scrawny nasturtium barely survived in its terra cotta pot; a legless white sofa and a glass coffee table shaped like a boomerang set on three mahogany legs faced the desk. Tricia Walter's desk was an antique, walnut French provincial table, its top a green marble inlay, certainly chosen to match the executive's eyes.

Her back to Jody, Tricia Walters sat in an old-fashioned wooden office chair and looked out the windows until the office door softly clicked shut, then Tricia Walters spun toward her, pointed to the potted palm and said, "I kill everything I try to nurture."

Her jeweled hand waved Jody to the legless white sofa, actually nothing more than cushions that folded back on themselves. Set on the ivory carpet, the sofa seemed solid as a cloud.

"So, Jody, without your dear father ready to speak for you, tell me, truly, how do you find school?"

Jody spoke for a while. She spoke truth. Why not? That was what courageous women did. What was there to lose? Her palm ran across the satiny white microfiber upholstery, smooth as skin.

Tricia Walters became a faceless silhouette against the window as the city fell into darkness. Rivulets of rainwater streaked the window glass. Once Jody exhausted her store of trivial college anecdotes, she went on to talk about her sense of isolation and the strangeness she felt around people her own age with whom she had next to nothing in common. Tricia Walters said nothing.

She had come to ask questions: she felt compelled to speak. She spoke true until she had no more to say.

After a little time, as if in exchange, Tricia Walters told Jody her own history. Ten years had taken her from peddling pinky rings rounded from bent silver spoons sold on street corners to being the branded genius behind Sultana Jewelry. Three years ago, she'd sold out to a consortium for an amount too staggering to be taken seriously, and far too much to be turned down. "One of the partners was with me for lunch," she explained. "Horrible man." For the coming decade they were obliged to pay her an obscene salary just to show up. Her only duty was to represent the firm at trade shows. She entertained customers. She no longer designed anything. To make her look good, the partners bought her clothes. "It's a tax write-off for the bastards." she said and laughed, "I buy the best I know how to buy."

So the two women circled the questions that could not be asked, the lives they'd never led, but might have. Was Cy Phillips a happy man? Was there a time I could have become your stepmother? Did you know my mother? Did she know of you? Are you the reason she drove her car into a tree? Instead, they talked politely about dorm food and how amber's luster was enhanced by the tiniest flaw when polished by flannel.

Longer and longer silences fell between them.

Jody slipped her shoulders out of her cardigan sweater, folded it, and placed it on the sofa beside her. The beret looked too smart to shed. When the intercom's red light blinked, Tricia Walters pressed a switch and said, "Nothing more."

Jody was only slightly surprised when the woman kicked off her shoes. They were inexpensive flats. She crossed her bare feet on her desk. Jody realized she was taller than Tricia Walters. "I suppose your father never mentioned me."

Jody remained mute.

"That's not surprising. There was not much to tell. By itself, our story is ordinary, maybe even sordid. Well, I assure you, the feelings between us were neither." When she spoke, the woman's ringed hands swooped like birds of paradise through the cone of white light shed by her desk lamp. Everything but those swooping hands, including Jody, was in darkness.

Jody felt her childhood drain from her, and was about to speak, when Tricia Walters said, "You can know this much. Your father asked me to join him for a cup of coffee a few times, I went, one thing led to another, and three months later we quit drinking coffee together. I was young, he seemed old, but the fact of the matter is we were both young." She withdrew a Balkan Sobranie cigarette, the paper black, the filter gold, from a drawer in her desk, and left the box in the lamp's spot of light. "I was about your age." Her butane lighter flared a globe of golden illumination on her face, but then her face returned to the shadows. Only the burning ember of her cigarette floated in the darkness. She added, "You'll also want to know I once lurked on a corner to spy on your mother. I had some idea I needed to confront her. Your father has no idea I ever did this. But she came out of the building where she and Cy lived with what looked like a ball of pink wool in her arms. That was you, of course. I froze. I'd come to settle something, but you intimidated me. Not your mother. You. You terrified me, Jody." Tricia Walters drew a long breath. "Your mother walked by me, a stranger on the street. I kept my eyes on your face. It's as close as I ever got to her."

"You were afraid?"

"I could no longer ignore the impropriety. You made me see myself for what I was, and it was nothing I ever thought I would be. I will tell you one thing, though. Happily married men don't find their way to other women's beds. But I did nothing, so I lost Cy. How stupid was that?"

"You never married?"

Tricia Walters said, "Let me tell you a story, Jody.

"Right after your father got the job in Minneapolis, that's a year or so after you were born, I joined the circus. I was stuck, and I needed to move on. The circus was an accident that came and took me away more than I sought it out. Once I'd figured out that college could only teach me how to work for somebody else, I quit. Your father had been my teacher. You must have figured that out. He was a graduate student, and I was taking History one-oh-one. Don't hate him. Cy is an honorable man who was unhappy and vulnerable, and I was very, very young and very forward. There was no question of a power relationship between us, no student-teacher thing. I did not exactly play hard-to-get. If you want details beyond that, Jody, you'll have to ask your father.

"I'd been selling my designs out of a suitcase on street-corners, at fairs. You know, the Feast of Saint This or The Blessed That. Fried sausages. Fried dough. Beer. And me, the little waspy kid who was a throwback to the sixties and sold trinkets. Everyone thought I was Italian. One of the fairs hired a carnival troupe, the guys with the rides and the fun houses, and I went with them. There was a pair of shoulders involved. He had this scar under his left nipple from a knife-fight, and the hair on his chest thick as a Karastan. I think I was twenty-two.

"The show made it to Rochester, New York, where the outfit self-destructed. Someone missed the rent on the rides. Gino vanished with a week's receipts. No one was paid. When we heard the Winslow Circus was in Buffalo, six of us crammed into a Chevy. Gonzo shoulders found work on a lake steamer; he set sail, and I never saw him again.

"Old man Winslow looked at me and said, 'Nice rack.' I smiled, and I had a job. A sweet old guy, he never tried anything, at least not with me. He liked pretty girls and he knew circus. One tent, one tiger, three clowns, eight horses, my two tits, and a baby elephant. Winslow put me to work in the sideshow. I bet I can still guess your weight within three pounds. One-eighteen?"

"One-sixteen."

"There you go. So one night The Amazing Mario, our knife thrower, comes to me and explains that his Loretta, his wife, partner, lover, mother of his three sons, and favorite target, is puking hard enough to lose her spleen. Bad mussels. Do I want to stand in? Catch a few knives?

"I tell Mario he is fucking crazy. What do I know about it? But he tells me I'm the only one with the chest to fit in Loretta's outfit. All I have to do is look pretty. He'll walk me through the act. In fifteen minutes, I tie back my hair—it was long, then—and I squeeze into Loretta's outfit, sequins, spangles, fishnet stockings so coarse you could pass goldfish through the mesh, a pom-pom on my ass, a rhinestone tiara with two-foot white ostrich feathers, and enough herring bone to shove my boobs over my head. You could set dinner service for two on my chest in that getup. I'd breathe when the act was finished.

"The music comes up—our orchestra was a tape-deck and big speakers, that's how rinky-dink Winslow's troupe was—Mario drags me by the hand, and the next thing I know I'm smiling at two hundred paying customers, my hands in the air, my feet in four-inch heels on sawdust, and Mario is juggling knives to the tune of "The Sabre Dance." In case you ever wondered, kid, I am here to tell you those knives are real. They weigh about four pounds each, nine inches of tempered steel. I smile and prance around, which it turns out is all I'm supposed to be doing. Mario turns me sideways, sticks a cigarette between my teeth, and like the breath of tomorrow a knife sails by. Thunk. It's in the wood backstop and I'm spitting tobacco shreds from my lips.

"Mario grabs my hand. We bow, and I am sure I have lost my mind because I have seen Mario and Loretta do this and I know what the finale is. We build to it. Mario throws knives with his lip. He throws knives with his foot. He throws knives backward. He throws knives upside-down through his legs. He throws knives standing on his head. He throws big knives.

He throws small knives. He throws straight knives, and he throws wicked little curved knives. Mostly what I do is hold up balloons and candles as targets when I am not pointing at Mario, milking the audience for more applause. I am smiling so hard my cheeks hurt, but a part of me that wants to run and hide. See, I know how this gig ends. I've seen Loretta ride the Wheel of Death.

"The act goes on and on, and when Mario cues the drum-roll, the house lights dim, two guys in white tights prance out, and they boost me onto the circular backstop.

"They strap me in. It's a grooved oak wooden disk, splintered where knives have bitten the wood. They fasten a leather strap across my waist, another at each ankle, and one more for each wrist. My arms are stretched over my head. The straps are stained dark, and I think how Loretta has sweated the leather black doing fourteen shows a week. I look like a rhinestone saint prepped for martyrdom. Joey the stagehand who will turn the wheel whispers to me to smile and not worry because all the stays are controlled by a single release. 'Anything happens, you're off in a minute,' Joey says as if this will reassure me, and he adds, 'Keep your eyes closed, kid, you'll be fine.'

"But I can't do that. I try, but my eyes pop right open. I'm not nervous. I'm excited. This is great! I think. This is the greatest thing that ever happened to me. They tilt the thing vertical and ignite sparklers all along the rim. Rubes never figure the flames are harmless. Look, you're in the center of a spinning wheel, fire is on the rim, centrifugal force is your best friend. The real danger is that the wheel stops before the fire is out.

"Mario begins to throw. Our shills in the audience start it off, but the rubes get the idea. They count. *One*, and Mario places the toughest knife early, before the thing spins too fast, right between my thighs. It quivers there as I slowly spin.

Then he slips on the blindfold. The boys spin the wheel faster. The world is whirling. The people in the seats are a blur, upside-down and then right side up. The tent lights spin around me. Colors run. Spotlights turn in orbits. Pink spots. Red spots. White spots. Music so loud, the bass vibrates through me. *Two. Three.* And more knives are in the wood, one at each side of my head. Mario begins to throw two at a time. I smile like a lunatic, all a target can do. I smell horse piss and the iron-stink of the sparklers, and I hear the creaks of the backstop's axle. Knives bracket my hips. The backstop spins faster and faster. I'm riding The Wheel of Death. Blood fills my head. I can't close my eyes. Knives surround my left ankle, but by now I am a marble in a kaleidoscope, and I don't hear the audience roar or count because it seems to me the colors make the noise. I'm at the bottom of a roaring whirlpool that is sucking in the rainbow. I think, *Am I screaming?* I want to, but can't. Screaming is not part of the act. People howl for us. The torches flare. The wheel is in a hot red spot. I never hear or see the knives that bracket my throat. I can't see a damn thing, just the colors whirling faster and faster, faster than the world goes round."

She paused and slowly lit a final cigarette. Her slim hand rested at the base of her delicate throat. "Jody, one night, I climbed onto the Wheel of Death and a mad Armenian threw knives at me. Why the hell would I ever need a husband?"

Jody laughed.

"But I tell you, kiddo, it taught me something."

"What's that?"

"Every woman is a target, kiddo. Get used to it. You may as well keep your eyes open. Take it all in. No one gets more than one chance on the wheel."

In the Arms of Men

Even as her feet were lifted from the ground by three men who bore her away to a rusted automobile parked curbside, motor running, doors gaping, a fourth man at the wheel, his gloved hand with fingers chopped bare gesturing that they hurry, hurry, man, hurry, even then, with their hands everywhere on her as she started to struggle, her elbow snapped hard against the soft flesh of one guy's neck, his short, surprised grunt of pain, his hand clamped around her wrist, arm pulled and twisted below and behind her, even then, as she was hoisted aloft, her wildly kicking feet hitting only air, a hand snatching at and enclosing an ankle, a gloved fist fouling her mouth with the taste of leather, wool and salt but failing to smother completely her scream, even then, Jody was startled by her sudden awareness of how long it had been since she'd known any touch other than the touch that came in the arms of men.

It was fifteen, no, sixteen years since her father's shoulder pressed into her stomach, the horizon going bump, bump, bump with each step he took down the knoll away from the heaps of flowers and the narrow trench where they left Mother. Daddy as he walked away saw what he saw, while Jody on his shoulder like a rolled carpet could see only backward, his shoulder compressing her so tightly that though her eyes watered, she had no breath for grief.

And even as her last, free sneakered foot found purchase against the car's roof and they tried to bend her into the automobile, even then she thought of how Bobby Williams when they were fourteen would actually pedal his dirt bike across half of St. Paul to the invisible place behind the tree in her backyard, the night so full of moon you could read a newspaper, and this Bobby would climb through her bedroom window and she would love him because he had the heart of a thief. Daytime, Bobby left her distracted for hours, whispering at lunch in the high school caf about a trick he'd seen in his Daddy's secret videos, making pictures in her mind so sharp that once when a geometry teacher had asked, "What are you thinking of?" she'd turned scarlet, blushing from her ankles to the tips of her ears, and everyone, everyone, knew exactly what she was thinking of, and that night Bobby bent her in angles that no geometry teacher could ever hope to know.

And even as she strained against the hand at the back of her neck, bending her head into the car, and even as she worked one hand free and she was able to pull at an ear, even then she thought how just two weeks before, in the Butler Library of Columbia University, she'd pondered Ibsen's *A Doll's House*, disgusted at how Nora's husband could behave like such a dickless chauvinist dipshit despite the fact that his wife who loved him had been ready to do the nasty with a slime-bucket blackmailer, when she looked up and saw across the table peering at her from beneath the green shade of the table lamp a man's aged two brown eyes. The eyes were dark as library furniture, eyes that radiated light.

"What?" she asked. "What? What?" and then she'd seen sadness pooling like honey in those eyes.

The owner of the eyes apologized. "I didn't mean to trouble you." She peeked at the title of his book. Statistics. Mother of God, a numbers-cruncher. He probably carried one of those fancy calculators, the kind where you touched a button and you got parabolas, a report on the Japanese stock market, and the weather in Zurich. When he carefully lifted a yellow highlighter and patiently ran it across the page, Jody couldn't help but compare her own study habit, which was to slash at the page with a #2 Ticonderoga pencil, jotting brilliantly into the margins of her books pithy little notes like, "Bullshit!" and "Oh yeah?" comments that admittedly proved less than helpful when she went back to read again before an exam.

"Now you are the one staring," he said. As he smiled, he lifted his rimless spectacles from his nose to rest on his forehead. He had a terrific smile. Great teeth. Even, white, the kind to take your breath away. Jody knew she was in trouble when she thought that since her own teeth were not so good, she would hope their children would inherit his teeth, not hers.

"I'm sorry," she said. "It's your highlighter."

"Do you want to borrow it?"

"It's how you use it. It's soothing."

Once again, Jody the Slow sounded as if she was on a day pass from the Home for Idiot Girls. Soothing?! Did she really say his highlighter was *soothing*?!

Walking together through cold rain to the West End Bar, she learned Damon was thirty-two, was pleased to be back at school full-time after three years of elementary school teaching, five years of marriage, and six months of divorce, all of it insignificant beside the fact that she felt within her something absolutely new, something that for her had no name and no precedent, something that had ridden on the aroma of wet wool emanating from his coat.

Here was a man shaped by sadness, so different from the boys she'd known, eager and shallow. Thirty-two, and gray was in his beard.

His apartment was redolent with pipe tobacco. Devastated by divorce, he owned only a three-legged sofa and a chair that bled stuffing. On a thin throw carpet on a hardwood floor, they drank Chianti and listened to Pavarotti until Damon said, "Angels. It's called 'Nessun Dorma.' The chorus sounds like angels." From the corner of Damon's closed eye a single tear trickled and vanished into the tangled curls of his beard.

He apologized for the display and walked her to the front of her dormitory. Their whole time together, he made no move toward her, never so much as touched her hand.

Unable to recall the melody that had moved Damon to a single tear, she sat through lectures and left with nothing but stark white notebook pages to show for her time. No professor could have said anything worth committing to paper. A red terry cloth band at her forehead, she ran through Riverside Drive to 79th Street and back, farther than she'd ever run, and still when she returned to her room, sweating and winded, she had so much energy that she dropped to the floor for fifty leg lifts and thirty push-ups, anything to make her body ache while her mind ran rampant. For days, she ran at twilight, the dark shadows of the high-rise buildings atop the New Jersey Palisades reaching across the Hudson, grasping shadow-fingers from the west. She pounded out sit-ups and crunches and threw up with abdominal pain, then did double sets of push-ups until she collapsed, nose against thin, ash-gray carpet.

And then, miraculously, he called.

At dinner, her teeth in a slice of pizza that blistered her palette, she breathed, "Take me with you."

"No," he said. They were quiet a time more.

Two days later, she walked to his apartment and taped a note to his door. Just her name and a question mark.

No more than a day after that, Jody was strangled by Othello. She was stretched over two plywood boards balanced on sawhorses. Her acting teacher said to her and the class, "Jody is where every woman goes when threatened by her husband. Her bed. It's where they have best known each other. It's where she has soothed him. It's where she has seen her warrior husband at his best and at his weakest. It's the only place she has any hope of being his physical equal, and so it the place that is her final hope. Jody will beg to live for a day, and she will be denied. She'll beg to live for half an hour, and her husband will deny her again. When she sees that nothing, nothing at all will save her, Jody's despair and terror will be absolute, and she will beg to live just for the length of a prayer, long enough for her to make her quietus with God, but her husband will even deny her that, too, in his rage willing to damn her."

Her teacher hopped onto their wooden bed and spoke directly to Jody, his leading lady for the day. "I have trusted you and you have betrayed me. You are innocent, faithful, devoted to me, your husband. You know all that, the audience knows all that, but I do not, and I am inflamed by jealousy and passion. You do not recognize me, the merciless warrior in your bed. The man you love, love with all your heart, is blind and deaf with fury at a betrayal you have not committed. Your head will be back, upside down off the side of the bed so the audience can share your death throes, and you're going to scream with horror. Can you give us a scream, Jody?"

He said, "Start with 'O banish me.'"

Her teacher's hands at her throat, her head hanging into space, him straddling her hips, her eyes rolling, his thinning hair dangling to her eyes, spittle drying at the corners of his lips as he bellowed Othello's accusations at Jody, his Desdemona of the day. His hands still on her, he civilly addressed the class, saying, "Your body is your instrument," and then without loss of a beat, switched back to raving.

"'Down, strumpet!'" He loomed over her. His eyes widened.

"'Kill me tomorrow: let me live tonight!'"

"'Nay if you strive,—'" He violently swung his leg over her chest. Startled, she wriggled beneath him, sliding half off the platform. Gravity slid her sweatshirt up her torso, exposing her back and ribs. The plywood board was rough against her bare back. A splinter of wood snagged in her bra.

"'But half an hour!'"

"'Being done there is no pause.'"

She held her bent knees together. "'But while I say one prayer!'"

The teacher bent close to her face, his pink-rimmed eyes wild, his thinning hair flying. He roared, "'It is too late!'" Spittle flew from his lips. His thumbs locked at her throat. Her head was a balloon filled with blood. His hands closed, and though she felt them tense, there was no real pressure. Her hands found his wrists. They were iron. Her legs thrashed. "Scream, kid," he hissed.

Nothing came.

He lifted her slightly, pushed her head back further, and that was when she felt the erection in his pants touch her hip. Her body was half off the wood. Her head nearly touched the stage. Her sweatshirt loosely fell about her neck, baring her from waist to her where her breasts strained to tumble from her bra. The keys dangling from her belt loop flipped up, icy against her bare skin. "Come on, kid, get this over with. Scream," he hissed through clenched teeth, and his thighs squeezed her hips.

Desdemona was innocent. The world was upside down, darkening as her vision blanked with blood, and from a place deep within herself once solid now molten, like a bubble formed a scream, expanding at her darkest center, below her belly, climbed the length of her spine, screwed tight her nipples and set her heart tripping as it rushed through her

chest, then gurgled up the narrowing cone of her throat until it erupted from her mouth, transforming as it blossomed
into the air into a flaming blackbird that flew from her lips.
Her entire body shuddered with its release. Her toes curled.
Her legs jerked rigid. She screamed again. Her vision faded
to complete black. She screamed a third and fourth time,
screamed until she had no breath. Heat filled her face. She
screamed until she was limp and the hands at her throat were
slippery with her perspiration.

"Perfect," the teacher said, and to the class's applause
lightly hopped to his feet and bowed.

That same night, Jody found Damon, and as a soprano
sang "Quando m'en vo' soletta," Jody took him on the three-
legged couch. Her teeth closed round the lobe of his ear. Her
fingernails raked his chest. Her breath rasped hot.

In the morning, by the thin light filtered through Damon's
bathroom's opaque window, in his mirror she examined the
red places on her hip, chest and throat where his beard had
rubbed her skin. A red welt lined her left breast. Her nipples
were sore. Two oval friction burns symmetrically framed the
small of her back. Rug burns spotted her knees. She dressed
quickly, left, and never awakened him, did not even kiss him
as he slept, looking too much like a boy, impossible to believe
that she'd have pressed so urgently back against him, eager,
audacious, flagrant.

Passion. The whole thing was entirely too dangerous.

So, soon afterward, when she saw Damon, her terror of
what was awakening within her left her no choice except to
hurry into a building and down a dim corridor that turned
and twisted away.

She fled through a miasma of formaldehyde and bolted
past heavy oak doors with bright lights shining over their

transoms, but by an open room where rabbits and rats scuttled in tiny cages, she heard, "Jody?" She hurled herself against a riot bar and tumbled through a doorway into a walled garden. Heart pounding, she climbed onto a concrete bench and then clambered over a brick wall, on the opposite side jumping to a pile of wet leaves. Breathless, she listened. Beyond the brick wall, a door creaked open and then sighed shut. It must have seemed to Damon that he'd pursued an illusion, and she felt like a craven little shit.

Which was why in her room she changed into running duds. She pulled on a knit hat, gloves, determined to circle the campus, Broadway to Amsterdam, 114th to 120th Streets. Four circuits. Maybe five. Cold air and exhaustion she is sure will burn her clean.

Half an hour later, perspiring freely, snugly hot within her clothes, breath smoking before her, she runs on the sidewalk through the early evening.

She runs east a fourth time on 120th Street with no trace of fatigue, certain she can finish six or seven circuits of the campus, darting from one pool of streetlamp light to the next. When a door of the lime green car springs open, it registers only as another obstacle to avoid. She moves diagonally across the sidewalk, closer to the buildings. The lime green car is old, a four door model, big as a yacht, its vinyl top peeled away to the unpainted metal beneath. Two men step from the car and cross the sidewalk before her. Their hands are in their pockets, their unbuttoned, long, gray coats flap at their knees. One man is black, the other is not. They walk directly to her, calm as though they will ask the time. She slows to avoid colliding with them, and a third man in the same coat comes from nowhere behind her, the car doors gape, and at that precise moment she understands her danger, but her momentum carries her into them. An arm blockades her chest; she bounces backward like a rubber ball.

Slow down, Speedy. What's your rush?

The weight of money is a nuisance. She has only her room key laced into her shoe. The third man closes her in. Her legs pump as though she still runs. They are a tiny circle around her. It is difficult to think. She wants only to run. There is no place to go. She wants to run.

We got us a girl. Check it out.

From behind, a hand wraps about her chest and through her two shirts and sweatshirt finds her breast. Across the street, people flow slowly down the stairs of Teachers College. The driver of the car—it is an Oldsmobile—waves *Come on* to his friends. That is when she thinks of her mother, how long it has been since she's known a woman's gentler hand. Automobiles pass on the street. Most have their headlights on, some do not. Nothing seems extraordinary. It is that time of evening.

We gonna have us a party.

You like to party?

They seem four friends met by accident on the street. Jody runs at them. The corral of arms does not yield. They laugh. She is caged. They start toward the car. She is caught in a moving box. As if she might be blind, someone takes her elbow.

She screams. A hand claps over her mouth, her head bends backward, her throat is exposed, a cry gurgles in her throat. Lifted by her knees, her feet leave the ground. Two arms circle her chest. She bobbed like this on Daddy's shoulder, the horizon bumping, him looking ahead, she behind. Hands on her, she is suspended in space, her head lower than her feet. Her mouth works free and she screams, less with terror than the sure knowledge that to be heard is her last, best hope. Her arm thrashes and slaps the bare metal car top. She strains, twists, and something pops in her arm, but she pushes against the roof with all her strength and desperation. Weight presses against her legs. She will snap in two. Bobby Williams made her feel as though she'd split and be something different afterwards. The car engine races. She kicks out and strikes something soft. A chest? They shout at each other.

Suddenly, she is dropped to the pavement. She lands on her hip. The Oldsmobile doors slam—one, two, three.

Her mittens are gone. Why would they steal her mittens? Her palms are skinned by sidewalk. Her knees bleed on cement. People from across the street run toward her. Boys in team jackets. An older man pulls at his trouser waist as he runs. Tires squealing, the Oldsmobile sideswipes a parked car, sprinkling shards of glass like wedding rice along the street. The car careens through a red light, fishtails, and vanishes.

A crowd circles Jody. She is on all her hands and knees as though searching for something, and directly before her eyes is a black-handled knife. Had she seen the knife, fear would have nailed her silent. She'd be in the car. She'd be gone. She'd be lost.

She struggles to stand. What did she do? an onlooker asks. Someone has kicked the knife away or picked it up. She touches her ear. It hurts. Her hat, a sad pile of wet wool by the curbstone where the Oldsmobile nearly swallowed her, lies in the street. When she moves toward her hat, the circle opens to let her pass. The hat's pom-pom hangs by a thread. The hat has been ground beneath someone's heel. The wool is dark where it is wet. When Jody bends, she becomes dizzy and reaches out to steady herself. When a man touches her hand, she whips hers back.

Blood in her nose bubbles. She limps toward Broadway. Pain sears her leg. Her knee is wrong. Well, no matter. She has sustained worse injuries. As Daddy would expect, she runs through injuries. She stretches her woolen hat low over her ears. Cold streetwater trickles down her neck, beneath her shirt collar. Where are her mittens?

Her knee works out. The pain lessens, but it will be worse tomorrow. Then it will get better.

When she wipes her runny nose with her wrist, it comes away smeared thick with mucous and blood. Testing herself, she runs a little harder, but it is too much.

The dorm desk clerk hardly notices her, and once upstairs in her room in darkness, on her only chair, the spare wooden thing they'd given her along with the desk, she sits and hugs her knees. When she becomes very cold she strips the blanket from her bed and wraps it about her shoulders. She shakes. Sweat dries to salt on her. Her nose runs, but then that stops. Sudden noises surge and retreat from her corridor. A cold, hard line of light steadily shines beneath her door. When a shadow passes, she trembles so hard she begins to weep. Why can't she control her own trembling?

Later, still in the perfect darkness, when the taste of blood is no longer metal on her tongue, she undresses. At the large hole in the knee of her sweatpants, blood has caked. Her sock is stiff with it. Grit covers her scraped palms. When she is sure she can be alone, in the shower stall furthest from the door, she stands beneath the hot water, her face to the spray, her eyes squeezed shut, staying far longer than she planned.

Pot

For years, Jody drifted at the perimeter of New York theater, but eventually she bored in to a niche as an administrator in a well-regarded regional company in western Massachusetts. She befriended playwrights and actors, and though she lived alone, that was just fine.

Her father's childless second marriage ended in acrimony. Jody was unsurprised, but she was sorry for Daddy's troubles. When a time came that he was to be honored by his university, Jody did the dutiful thing. At the airport gate, as his arms enfolded her, through his coat's bulk her hands immediately felt precisely why his colleagues hastened to grant the honors ordinarily reserved for a man more senior.

At his home, a condo, neither the house where Jody had grown up nor the farmhouse where he'd lived with Sarah, Daddy poured Portuguese brandy as Jody set a hardwood fire. The alcohol warmed her; he hardly touched his to his lips. He whirled the snifter. "Pancreatic cancer," he said, "I can live with it." And he smiled wanly as his prepared joke fell flat and his Jody-girl cried anyway.

The day after the testimonial dinner, Jody phoned her employer. It was no trouble in winter to release her for a month more.

Brandy before the fire became a ritual. Jody told her father about her career and the occasional man who visited her life, none special. Yes, she thought herself as fulfilled as she could be.

Daddy listened, his head nodding, falling to his chest, jerking upright, his fluttering eyelids losing the struggle until he slipped into sleep, his legs wrapped in Canadian blankets. Pain was exhausting.

"You need to know about your mother," he said the week before Jody's life required her return to the details of living. He was chasing her away, refusing to allow her to be near during what they both knew would be a difficult, painful and ultimately fruitless round of treatments. She'd privately wept, made secret arrangements with a doctor to keep her informed, but otherwise did not argue with him.

"We were part of a circle of friends, mostly men, boys, really, younger than you are now. Dating. We were students. She still lived with your grandparents. I lived alone. We played cards, poker mostly, but sometimes bridge or hearts.

"Your mother was a tough card player. She never partnered with me at bridge because she knew she'd be furious with me if we lost. Losing was unacceptable." He laughed until he coughed, recovered, and continued.

"The end of one night we got a little punchy, a little crazy, and so someone dealt acey-deucey. Do you know the game?"

Jody shook her head.

Daddy sighed. "In poker you bet as you go, a certain amount each card, and you play against the other players. But in acey-deucey you play against the pot. Everyone puts up one dollar. The pack is shuffled, two cards are turned face up to each player in turn, and the player bets any amount up to the whole pot that the next card will fall between the first two. The best chance is an ace and a deuce, the highest and lowest cards."

Jody nodded. It made no sense to her, but the details did not matter.

"Some hands simply cannot be won. You can't draw a third card between a five and a six, for example, but you still have to make a minimum bet. So the game can go forever because there's a player who never gets tired—the pot. If you decide to go home, even if everybody decides to go home, who owns the money in the middle of the table?

"That night the cards were treacherous. Someone would be dealt a king and a four, bet five dollars on what seemed a sure thing, and the next card would turn up a three. Four separate times a player was dealt ace-deuce, called *pot*, which meant they bet the whole thing, and lost because another ace or deuce turned up. A tie doesn't win this game. The pot doubled, doubled, and doubled again. We became grim. Lots of smoke. Quiet. Just the snap of the cards.

"Your mother was dealt the King of Hearts and the Trey of Clubs. She said, 'Pot,' right away, didn't even think about it, didn't count the money to see if she could cover her bet. That was her way. But the fellow who was dealing the cards, Bill, didn't turn the next card over. Instead, he said, 'Where's your money?'

"Your Mom laughed. She had a wonderful laugh. She thought Bill was joking. "I'll write you an I.O.U.,' she said.

"'Nothing doing,' Bill said. You see, if he could make your mother bet less than the whole thing, why then he and the other players still had a chance at the money. They insisted your mother either have the money or bet less. They counted it. One hundred and twelve dollars. A lot of money for us then. I didn't have enough to lend to her.

"'All right,' she said. 'I'll get it.' She said to me, 'Phillips, watch that deck of cards,' swung on her jacket and charged out the door. We heard her car start and her tires squeal down the street. Two o'clock in the morning, your mother went out into the night while we stared at each other and the tiny pack of cards at the table's center.

"Forty-five minutes later, she returned. Her hair drooped over her eyes and she had six twenty-dollar bills in her fist, her coat collar was around her ears, and the final stub of a cigarette was between her thumb and index finger. Her eyes were marbles. She must have gone to her father, awakened him, told him the story, and he'd given her the money— he was a sport, your grandfather, but to ask him for a loan must have cost your mother a lot, a lot more than money. She'd spent her whole life, trying to prove to herself and the world that she was not 'Daddy's little girl.' I don't suppose you know anyone like that, do you?"

Daddy's laugh bubbled into a wet cough. He pulled his blankets tighter around his legs. Staring into the fire, he spoke slowly, savoring the memory being replayed before his eyes in the flames.

"She ground her cigarette into an ashtray, slapped the bills down on the table and said, 'Pot. The whole damn pot.' Bill turned up a nine.

"Your mother didn't smile. Like she expected it, was entitled to it, knew it all along, and was angry with us for requiring her to demonstrate what was so plainly fated to be. She stuffed money into her pockets. Your mother never carried a purse, but she toted a wallet in her back pocket, like a man.

"And then she left as abruptly as she'd returned. We heard her car engine start, her tires squeal once more, and we were left to look at each other.

"That night I knew I'd have to marry her. I needed her strength. You know, I am weak, Jody. You know that, don't you?" He stared into the dying fire. "'No skid marks' they said. No skid marks, my ass."

At the end, she was summoned back. She did what she could do, which was nothing at all. That was very hard.

Soon after, among Daddy's final effects Jody found a sealed cardboard crate, one side crumpled from the weight of book cartons that had rested on top of it. The box smelled of mildew and age. Sitting cross-legged on the concrete floor of a rented storeroom, she peeled the masking tape from the seams.

Photographs. Several of her mother holding the infant Jody. Jody saw that the older her mother had become, the less frequently the camera found her smiling. Here, her mother laughed at a boat dock. There, she was as a teenager at what might have been summer camp. But a later photo at some picnic showed her mother's ongoing annoyance gathering like a storm; her hand holding a burning cigarette extended before her to obstruct the camera. In the background, Jody, maybe two, wore a denim jumpsuit and, barefoot, played with her pink feet.

Her mother had not been a happy woman, but the photos offered Jody no deeper clues. By the time Jody's mother was Jody's age, her mother was dead.

She'd outlived her. It was finished. Jody need not recapitulate her mother's life.

Beneath the photographs, Jody uncovered her mother's letters. The historian could discard no written record. She riffled the pack; the letters were in chronological order. Jody read three adolescent gushing avowals of perpetual devotion, became embarrassed, and returned the three letters to their place in the pack. Then, so she'd never be tempted to look again, she tossed everything except one photo of her and her mother into the fireplace.

It was easier to do than she could have imagined.

Daddy's ashes scattered, Jody drove her father's newest Buick—now hers—to the cemetery in St. Paul. She could no longer avoid the obligatory visit. It was time to make peace.

Her mother's grave was not well tended, though wild purple and white alyssum in the spare grass gave the site a settled look. She'd brought no flowers, wished she had, and promised herself that she would when next she returned, even as she acknowledged no such time would ever occur. The Midwestern August air was laden with the familiar smell of dust and cut hay. The high sun cast sharp shadows. Lowering herself to one knee, her fingertips traced the shallow letters etched in the smooth marble—Samantha Kaufman Phillips, Loving Mother.

Hours later, driving east, for no reason she understood, she steered the Buick off the interstate. She found herself on a parallel road, a winding two-lane blacktop lined on each side by pines. Her mother had died on a road very like this.

A summer storm mounted behind her. On a long straight-away, air-conditioning off, windows down, Jody accelerated. Fragrant summer air cooled by the trees' shadows washed over her. The Buick gathered speed. The roar of passing air became thunderous. The unchanging, uncluttered horizon rushed faster and faster toward her without drawing any more near, while beside her what had been individual trees blurred to solid, narrowing walls.

Jody gently closed her eyes. She lifted her hands from the steering wheel. She listened to her blood.

She was a leaf, a leaf afloat on surging waters that rushed through a steep flume. The exhilarating plunge quickened her heart. Her foot pumped the accelerator. Her eyes closed, the world was dark and grew darker, but she felt a presence, and then her eyes bolted open as the car shot forward from shadow into the dazzling light beyond the trees onto a vast rolling plain that stretched to the farthest horizon.

— with thanks to sjl

Danger

Rockaway Parkway begins near the sand beaches beside the darkest reaches of Jamaica Bay in Queens, New York. On a summer night in 1967, Marsha and I cruised in search of hitchhikers. Stupid, but we were bored, and this seemed like a clever way to pass the time. This is two years before we marry, have our kid, divorce, float around the country, remarry, have more kids with other people, bury parents, rest and recover at an institution, start again, acquire chemical habits, commit adultery, contemplate suicide, bail our kid out of jail, crack up a car and a knee in Pennsylvania, quit those chemical habits, earn graduate degrees, default on a loan, outlive our molars, try to reverse a vasectomy, are treated for skin cancer, suffer heart palpitations, have the hernia operation, consider tubal ligation, start the blood pressure meds, quit the Pritikin diet, tip off a motorcycle, feel ridiculous making a pass at that young kid, discover the simple pleasures of frozen yogurt, and feel triumphant awakening beside that other young kid.

Marsha's boxy Rambler's seats reclined horizontally, a setting Marsha and me in a pre-Orthonovum age made rare use of. Rat brown, a frozen locked rear door on the passenger side, it accelerated from 0 to 60 in less time than it takes to grow a mature sycamore. Despite a coat hanger jammed in the socket where the buggy-whip antenna had been snapped off, the radio played. FM rock radio was new.

Near Rockaway Playland, the Ferris Wheel washed the streets with neon blue, neon green, and neon yellow light. In the garish glow, everything looked two weeks dead. Our first hitchhiker was a thick-lipped boy who fell into the Nash's rear seat like a man grown accustomed to something breaking his falls. He rolled his eyes and his head leaned back, and in the rearview mirror I saw his Adam's apple bulging in his throat, his skin luminous and slick as a trout's belly.

Though I'd never been west of Hackettstown, New Jersey, in my best Oklahoma drawl I said, "How y'all doin'?"

"Real good," our rider said. "I just need to go a few blocks."

"We've been livin' on the beach," Marsha said. "We're out from Denver. We're on the road."

We'd been devouring Kerouac. We could eat chili dogs, too. Jesus, the things we could digest.

Our guy rolled down his window, put his face into the wind, and threw up. He threw up full bore, threw up with every muscle of his body, kneeling on the rear seat, his legs quivering like a wet dog's. After a while he said, "I feel better now," and wiped his lips on his shirtsleeve. We were grateful he'd had the presence of mind to put his head out the window. I figured to hose the car, later, and I was glad it was the door, and not the window, that was frozen.

When he tapped the back of my seat, we stopped, and he lurched off into the darkness.

"That was hardly Montana Slim," Marsha said. "I don't think we impressed him."

Marsha had truly black eyes. Her hair was lustrous and long. She never tweezed her eyebrows, and the hairs grew so thick they merged just above her nose. Her complexion was sallow, and she was hollow-cheeked, a kind of wasted, tubercular look that at that time was the sign of the seriously concerned, deeply politicized, thoroughly committed and, therefore, very sexy woman. Think Joan Baez. These days, our daughter looks like Marsha did then, though she thinks of her appearance as a curse. Fashions change. That shadowed night, with sparks of amber and green from the dashboard reflecting highlights in her hair, the smell of stale crushed cigarettes from the Nash's ashtray and the faint stink of puke about us, with the thick heat of the July night, the radio tuned to WNEW-FM with Allison Steele, The Night-Bird, as far as we knew the first female disk jockey, a woman who started every show with some cosmic intonation ending with the words, "Come, fly with me," and who then played the sonorous break from "Court of the Crimson King," with all that, how could I have imagined Marsha would bear me a child who would when she was fifteen request in the same tone as she did my help with algebra ask for a face lift? I ask you, how could I have imagined that?

We carted high school girls who thought that it was psychedelic that we had hitched from Denver and lived on the beach. They were considering going to San Francisco. Everyone was. Scott McKenzie sang on every radio. One girl asked us where we went to the bathroom. Another asked if we begged for food or worked for it. This is 1967; those were ordinary questions. Thinking of Henry Fonda, I told them we stole food, and they said, "Outta sight." We gave a lift to a couple who were simply tired of waiting for the bus. Marsha and I made up stories.

But we were tired of our game and about to head home when we picked up a kid right in front of Playland. He looked beat, which was just how we wanted him to look, and he looked broke, which made him perfect. Rockaway Parkway isn't Route 66. You make do.

Marsha told Duke our story about running east in Colorado, coasting down out of the Rockies into Denver without gasoline. Duke asked, "Where'd you get a car with New York plates?"

So Marsha invented a cousin who'd loaned it to us. That first car, she said, broke down in Ohio. We'd hitchhiked from Cleveland. But Duke asked why if we had a cousin in New York who'd loan us a car, we still had to live on the beach. Marsha lighted a Marlboro and offered one to Duke, who took it. One-handed, he snapped open a metal Zippo. Blue flame fluttered, we smelled lighter fluid, and then the lighter clicked shut. Marsha asked why Duke needed to thumb a ride.

"I was out with the guys, you know? And they wanted to boost cars. I don't need that. You get busted, you're in a world of shit."

I adjusted the mirror. All I saw in back seat was the smoldering tip of his cigarette.

"You ever been busted?" I asked.

"Only once. Those assholes boost cars all the time. But tonight I said, 'Not Duke,' and when Gino called me a pussy, I showed him this."

I heard the slide of a mechanism. Switchblade? Gravity knife? I'd never seen either, but when he reached around me in the front seat, by the light of passing cars I saw the glint of steel, maybe seven inches long, maybe eighteen, maybe a damned machete. The blade turned toward my throat.

Marsha knelt on the front seat, her behind toward the windshield. "Nice knife," she said as Duke's arm withdrew into the darkness.

I remember being fearless, which is not the same as having courage, and I am sure Marsha felt the same way. I have felt fear since then. Take that time on the Illinois Interstate when a car silent as a yacht in a dream crossed the median and floated at seventy miles per hour a few feet in front of my hood, cut a swath through the high yellow grass beyond the road bed, and plunged over a drainage ditch through a barbed wire fence and into a tree to crash with a sound that had more finality than any I have heard since. We stopped, but there was nothing to be done, and since I was again traveling to a new job and yet another new life, I continued on my journey. Thirty minutes farther on when I could no longer hold the wheel, I stopped on the shoulder and waited for my shakes to quit.

But that night on Rockaway Parkway I had no knowledge of loss and so no sense of fear. We were nineteen and immortal. Separated from my shoulder blades by a few inches of springs covered by vinyl upholstery and cheap stuffing, a desperado named Duke smoked Marsha's cigarette and toyed with a blade long enough to pass through the driver's seat, my cotton workshirt, my skin, my ribs, and tickle a major organ.

We stopped, Duke thanked us, folded his knife, and was swallowed by the vastness of a Queens summer night.

For Marsha and me, it was a totally satisfactory evening.

The Gremlin Theory of Personality was explained to me in one of those restaurants with brass junk and enamel flour sack ads hung on dark wood walls. Rattan fans spun near the ceiling, and "singles" on high stools sipped trendy wine at the bar. Richie, the guy who explained the Gremlin Theory, had been a Navy Seal in Vietnam. This conversation was in Kansas, as far from ocean as you can get, several years after the last helicopter lifted off from a roof in Saigon.

All you've heard about neuroses, psychoses, trauma—it's all crap. The Gremlin lurks dormant at the back of your skull. As long as the Gremlin sleeps, you go about your business like a citizen. But when things are too smooth, alarms go off. The aroused Gremlin assumes command, and you are helpless. You confuse your dick with a compass and follow wherever it leads; you sleep with your best friend's wife. You take a second mortgage and place a very serious wager on a seriously lame horse. Suddenly, you decide that the nine to five job that pays you excellent money leaves you unfulfilled; what you resolve to do is to surf or some such shit.

Richie's wife was devoted to him. After two children, her figure still left men dry-mouthed. Richie had literary ambitions, and his wife was content to leave him daily at the roll-top antique oak desk she bought for him and had refurbished before it went into their finished basement. Over the years, she rose to become branch manager of one of the banks in that Kansas town; Richie enjoyed mild literary success. He wasn't going to be famous, but no one could accuse him of being a hobbyist, either. This entirely satisfactory arrangement evaporated the weekday afternoon their daughter, a high school junior, discovered Daddy and her classmate on a living-room couch engaged in a sex act that is still illegal in Tennessee.

"The Gremlin," Richie said and shrugged, pushing his Detroit Tiger hat back over his balding head and tugging his ear.

No one ever got Richie's war story straight. He wouldn't talk about it, and there was no telling from the adventure novels he wrote how much was true and how much was not. Dead honest lies he called the paperbacks he ground out. Shrapnel wounds had transformed Richie's back into a terrain map, and people who ought to know told me tales about weeks on some jungle river, wounded comrades, eating insect protein, infection, fever, a five-mile swim through coastal waters, and a Silver Star that would have been a Medal of Honor if more witnesses had lived.

Long before the guy twenty years her senior proposed to my daughter, before the kidney stones and the ectopic pregnancy, before the credit crunch and the bankruptcy hearing, long before the lithium and the afternoon on the hotel-room-window ledge eight stories above San Francisco, in the days when a six transistor radio was better than a four transistor radio, and music stores sold vinyl records, back when people dialed telephones by actually turning a wheel, when I was seventeen, even before Marsha, long before I ever heard of male pattern baldness, soon after the Cuban Missile Crisis, but before Reagan invaded Grenada, when the Shah ruled Iran, inflation was an event in the life of a balloon, and Saddam Hussein was a nomad, Cathy was my girlfriend.

The Friday night after Thanksgiving, I borrow Dad's Chevy Impala. I forget where we went. It was cold, very cold, and when I drive Cathy home she asks me to park a little bit up the street so we can talk, which for that time and that place is code that means we will not talk at all. I do not mean to sound sinister. It was very innocent, really. Cathy and I kiss clumsily, our teeth clicking like a bad transmission. I am amazed when she moves my hand here, and then there, her body pressing against my wrist and my forearm. We are smothered under our clothing; mittens, mufflers, knit hats, Cathy's with a red pompom. There's my sweater. There's Cathy's sweater. We wear stadium coats, heavy woolen hooded things with wooden toggles and tiny leather loops. We wear penny loafers and sweatsocks, we wear striped scarves, and, come to think of it, we both wear Oxford white shirts with button-down collars. Everything but our underwear is identical, even the lengths of our hair.

We do as much as we have the courage to try with our clothes on, but everything is opened, unfastened, unsnapped, undone, or untied. Women's slacks had zippers anywhere but the front. Cathy teaches me the excitement of a tongue tip in an ear. When her eyes squeeze shut and she leans into me, her breath rasping, I hold her tightly as she quakes, and hope I've done nothing wrong. Cathy is a year older than I. Inside my pants is a mess.

The car windows mist opaque with our breath. After I walk her to her door, before I can drive, I scrape ice off the inside of the window. As soon as I am home, I telephone her. At 3:00 A.M., we whisper beautiful nonsense.

The next Friday, after a movie, Cathy invites me to climb the long flight of red brick steps of her parents' house. She leaves me in what she calls the TV room, tells her parents that she is home safely, and then returns to me. The room is windowless, tiny. A television, an armchair with plaid covered cushions, a daybed, and a few plants. Cathy must have had an agreement with her parents; short of the house being on fire, in that room, we could not be disturbed.

Every weekend, and then every night during Christmas recess, by the flickering blue light of terrible black and white horror films, as Godzilla or one of his mates stomps Tokyo into rubble, in the small hours of the morning we peel off each other's clothing. Our excitement is impossible to describe. One night, someone moves in the kitchen. Cathy freezes like a spooked deer, but after a few minutes, the noise stops and we resume even more excited by the interruption. We engage in any activity that allows Cathy to maintain her technical virginity, a restriction that left us to choose from an incredible array of activities and contortions. We were young, tireless, and must have been very pretty together.

I thought only of three things. First, myself—I won't kid you. Second, Cathy. And third, from time to time I'd consider how Cathy's parents might at any moment burst through the lockless door.

All that kept us from discovery was Cathy's trust. Now I can suppose that they believed that a young man with their daughter in a windowless room under their roof was preferable to their daughter with a young man in an automobile God alone knew where, but then and there, for me the risk of discovery was exhilarating. Cathy writhed in my arms while I knew her parents were just beyond an unlocked hollow wood door. What could they think we were doing until two, three, and four o'clock in the morning? I began to believe I was violating her, violating her whole family, shredding the fabric of civilized behavior, and I understood why, for all of human history, rape of a bested adversary's women has been a prize of conquest. The fantasy charged me, made me bold, and I think

Cathy loved that. In truth, I love her memory now more than I did her body then.

Those nights, Cathy gave me my first cigarettes. I enjoyed the ritual. We'd fall on each other, and then we'd rest, sated, smoking Parliaments from a blue and white soft pack. We'd stare at each other's nakedness while we shared an ashtray in the center of the day bed, and then we'd irresistibly stroke each other, smoke a little, touch a little more, and then find ourselves unable to stay apart. Smoke curled lazily about us. The recessed filter was elegant, clean. I remember coughing, and I remember Cathy smiling at me until I got it right, and I remember how the whole time while I admired my own sophistication and the style with which I inhaled and then tapped an ash, I was thinking that the greatest risk I ran was the fury of her father next door.

Now do you see what I'm saying?

This is completely Marsha's story. I wasn't even there. Still, it makes a point.

We believed that to know was to control. Not just Marsha and I. Everyone. You think not? How many people do you know who have again and again tried to reassert control of their lives by enrolling in school, pursuing yet another advanced degree or certification, any course of study that guaranteed a measure of expertise? Marsha shared this illusion. She periodically "retooled." Somehow, she wound up in the "helping professions," a natural outcome of her interest in "the human potential movement." She became employed in "human services."

Let me take the shine off. Marsha ran group encounter sessions at the town's drunk tank, a coed residential program. Given the choice of thirty days in the county lockup or three months in the county rehab, your average street drunk will opt for rehab. There was a clean shirt in it, the food was better, and with luck an inmate might get laid. Once in a while, I'd volunteer some hours at reception or driving the drunk tank's van, and so I came to know a few of the regulars—guys with serious problems. I learned that if a fluid burns blue you probably could drink it, but if it burns bright red, watch out.

Marsha was very good at what she did. She could walk through the toughest parts of town at any time of night and no one dared lay a hand on her. She was safe because on any given corner, there was sure to be two or three guys who had told the skinny lady about their kids or their mothers. Their souls exposed raw, they'd wept in front of her, and so they would make damn certain that anyone who might harm Marsha would at least lose a kneecap, maybe even get gut stuck.

One day while Marsha conducts a group session, her phone rings. One of her discharged clients, Charlie, calls long distance. He is home in North Carolina, but he needs to talk to Marsha right away, a matter of life and death.

It was Marsha's policy to take no calls during sessions, especially from clients. For one thing, it was unfair to members of the group. For another, the psychopathology of addictive personalities is such that to allow instant gratification is an error, and so a good therapist doesn't drop everything and run to the telephone just because a client is demanding attention from the other end. The switchboard operator takes Charlie's number. Two hours later, Marsha calls him back.

She'd been fond of Charlie. He left the rehab program detoxed in body and spirit, and so Marsha expects to hear a success story from a guy just touching base. But that is not the case. No. Charlie needs to talk to Marsha, all right. He has his Browning Automatic, the .45, and the good news is that he is not suicidal, but the bad news is that his parents are bound with lamp wire, gagged, propped up on the couch in the living room, and they watch baseball with Charlie while they wait for Marsha's return call.

As Charlie learned in group, being up-front is the most important manageable aspect of a man's life, and Charlie had come to the conclusion that his father's and mother's brains need to be spattered onto the wall. That is as up-front as he knows how to get. He has caused them considerable pain in their lives, for which he is truly sorry, and he wishes to cause them no more, so a neat one behind the ear is his plan. First his old man, who deserves it more, and then Mom. What does Marsha think?

Marsha apologizes for taking so long to get back to him. She regrets the delay, and she swears to Charlie that had she known of the matter's urgency, she'd have hurried through group session. Charlie understands, having been in group himself. He figures it was something like that, so suspecting he was on his own, he decided to carry out his plan at the baseball game's end even if Marsha did not call. He guessed it was his parents' good luck that the score is tied and they are in the bottom of the tenth with Atlanta having just left men on first and third.

Marsha waves wildly to her staff, scribbling notes on any piece of paper she can find. On another line, they phone the North Carolina highway patrol, and the chief administrator of the drunk tank actually has to hang up and allow the state-trooper barracks to call him back because they are sure the call is from a crank. The delay absorbs five minutes. They dig out Charlie's initial registration card to learn his home address in North Carolina. The state troopers call a county sheriff.

Think of this: Charlie calls Marsha in Arizona, Marsha calls the North Carolina state police, the state troopers call a local sheriff. Information is circling the country. The sheriff wants to know about Charlie. Has he made any demands? Did he have any other weapons? Which room of the house is he in? Front or back? Her boss is whispering these questions to Marsha, and Marsha is trying to connive such details from Charlie without alerting him that the county-mounties are burning rubber off the tires of three cars hurtling down back roads in a Code 3, sirens, lights and pedal to the metal. Those good ol' boys have donned Teflon flak jackets and are loading riot guns. They wish they owned a helicopter, what with Charlie's folks' place way the hell back in the woods, but they are getting ready for this turkey shoot on the ground.

Thirty minutes pass while Marsha and Charlie weigh the pros and cons of murder as a therapeutic device. Charlie is not stupid, just crazy, and he completely accepts the consequences of his act. He knows just how he will feel afterward, and he is sure he will be able to handle it, and, yes, he expects to be arrested and punished and to do hard time, but he expects to suffer the consequences of his actions, a lesson he learned in Marsha's group sessions.

Marsha is frantic to keep Charlie talking, but when the baseball game ends with a two-run homer in the bottom of the thirteenth inning, Charlie says he has to do what he has to do, and Marsha hears the telephone receiver clatter to a tabletop. She screams Charlie Charlie Charlie, calling his name as loud as she is able, screaming at the people she works with to tell the sheriff to put a fire under it, and then she hears a gunshot, Bang, so loud her ear on the telephone hurts. Then she hears another shot, Bang, just as loud, and then, after what seems like forever but in fact is no more than a few heartbeats, she hears a third. Her head rings. She is dry-mouthed and faint. She shifts the telephone to her un-numbed ear but hears only the faint, distant murmur of the post-game show.

This is the moment when on the other telephone line the sheriff's men in North Carolina report via the state trooper's dispatcher that they are arrived at Charlie's parents' address, a mobile home set on cinder blocks in a pine forest. They burst through the locked front door with their guns drawn to roust a half-naked man and wife asleep in their bedroom. They did have a son, Charlie, but they have not heard from the worthless son of a bitch in two years, so what the North Carolina sheriff wants to know is whether the folks that had sent them on this damn wild goose chase could please take their heads out of their asses and explain what in hell was going on. Running around with drawn shotguns can get a civilian killed.

Marsha yells into her telephone, "Charlie, you bastard!" and Charlie, of course, picks up his end and says, "Gotcha!"

When Marsha told me this story, she thought it was funny. This was very soon before the divorce, though Marsha had already decided. She had a lover by then. It was some time after the birth of our son, the one who didn't live, and it was considerably before the accident that took the dog, the burglary that got the stereo, the silver and the coin collection, and it was long, long before anyone ever heard of Mogadishu or thought 9-11 was anything but a date in late summer.

One last.

I was neither happy nor unhappy, waiting for things to start again. A job had ended. Another job would begin at the summer's end. Such are the rhythms of a teacher's life.

At a rock concert scheduled for a field near a dragstrip, a half dozen bands will gather to play for a day and a night. A mini-Woodstock. I thought it would occupy me, bring back lost times. I'd sit in the sun, surround myself with thousands of younger people, they'd ingest drugs and drink beer, we'd listen to music that was new when I was, and I'd brood on the decline of the West.

The day dawned glorious. At ten in the morning, I park two miles from the concert site. Lined with cars on the shoulders, the single lane blacktop road is choked with people trekking to the dragstrip's grounds. They carry coolers and backpacks. At noon, the concert begins. The sun is strong. High, white clouds dot the blue sky, the music is passable, and a group of people, kids really, invite me to join them, share their food and wine, and sit on their blankets. I wish I'd thought to bring a hat. The air is cool, but the strong sun heats my flannel shirt. When I take off my shirt, a young girl sits so close beside me our hips touch. She tells me she thinks gray chest hair is cool.

The concert is less a demonstration of music than a celebration of community. In this field, we are one.

Late in the afternoon, between bands, a small aircraft buzzes overhead. Small planes have passed above us all day; journalists, I assumed. But this airplane is lower and more insistent, circling tightly, very low, and people all over the field begin to take notice. When at the height of a loop the plane emits a plume of white smoke, we know it must be part of the show. Can it herald the next band?

Sure of our attention, the plane climbs, slows, and then the sharpest-eyed among us see the parachutist leap from a door behind the wing. The girl beside me points. The parachutist plummets like a stone for a few seconds, and then his parachute blossoms. Everyone on the field applauds, but we rise to our feet to cheer when he ignites red, white and blue smoke bombs. The three colors spiral about him as he twists in the wind. Great plumes of colored smoke stain the sky. People whistle, stomp their feet, and shout. It is a magnificent moment.

Only the next day do we learn from newspaper accounts that the rogue parachutist had nothing to do with the show. In fact, his nylon jumpsuit caught fire from the three smoke bombs strapped to his waist. He'd been aflame, burning right before our eyes, dead before he touched the ground. Unable to know his pain, as he twisted and spun above us we cheered every foot of his agonized descent. We hollered and shouted, oohed and aahed through the nightmare of his slow, excruciating final fall to the earth, in our ignorance thrilled by his exquisite beauty.

Perry Glasser's stories have won the PEN Syndicated Fiction Prize three times and the Boston Fiction Festival twice. He is the author of two prior fiction collections: *Suspicious Origins*, which won the Minnesota Voices Award (New Rivers Press) and *Singing on the* Titanic (University of Illinois Press). A former public high school English teacher in New York City, after years of being a magazine editor, he currently coordinates the Professional Writing program at Salem State College in Massachusetts.